THE IMPORTANCE

OF HIGH PLACES

THE IMPORTANCE
OF HIGH PLACES

STORIES AND A NOVELLA

by JOANNA HIGGINS

MILKWEED EDITIONS / MINNEAPOLIS 1993

Milkweed Editions
528 Hennepin Avenue, Suite 505
Minneapolis, Minnesota 55403-1810
Books may be ordered from the above address.

ISBN 0-915943-79-4
97 96 95 94 93   5 4 3 2 1

Publication of Milkweed Editions books is made possible by grant support from the Literature Program of the National Endowment for the Arts, the Cowles Media / Star Tribune Foundation, the Dayton Hudson Foundation for Dayton's and Target Stores, Ecolab Foundation, the First Bank System Foundation, the General Mills Foundation, the Honeywell Foundation, the I. A. O'Shaughnessy Foundation, the Jerome Foundation, The McKnight Foundation, the Andrew W. Mellon Foundation, the Minnesota State Arts Board through an appropriation by the Minnesota State Legislature, the Northwest Area Foundation, the Beverly J. and John A. Rollwagen Fund of The Minneapolis Foundation, the Lila Wallace-Reader's Digest Literary Publishers Marketing Development Program, and by the support of generous individuals.

Library of Congress Cataloging-in-Publication Data

Higgins, Joanna.
  The importance of high places : stories and a novella / by Joanna Higgins.
  p. cm.
  ISBN 0-915943-79-4
  I. Title.
PS3558.I3574I47 1992
813'.54--dc20   92-41957
                              CIP

ACKNOWLEDGMENTS

I would like to thank the National Endowment for the Arts for a Fellowship grant in 1989 and also thank my excellent "first readers" these past years, Virginia Sheret, a great good friend, and my husband Jerry, for their critical comments and unbounding encouragement. I'm most grateful to Emilie Buchwald and the staff of Milkweed Editions, as well, for the care taken with these words. Special thanks, also, to John Covelli for inspiring "Opening Day." And finally, I must acknowledge the late John Gardner, without whom these words would not be.

"The Courtship of Widow Sobcek" first appeared in *MSS* (Spring 1981) and later in *The Best American Short Stories 1982* (Houghton Mifflin, 1982).

"Dinosaurs" first appeared in *American Fiction IV* (Summer 1992).

"The Importance of High Places in a Flat Town" first appeared in *Prairie Schooner* (Spring 1987).

for my husband

FOUR STORIES:

A NOVELLA:

four stories

OPENING DAY

Mountains blurred with fog, a forecast for more damp and raw weather on opening day, and Dieter Jahnke was glad. Let it be foggy, let it sleet, let there be an ice storm, let the clouds plop right down into the woods and stay there. And let these thoughts fly straight from his heart to the ear of the Almighty, who somehow saw fit to allow such atavistic lapses as deer hunting. Each November, the mountains gray and brushy, the sodden hay fields a fading ocher, the overcast low and tumbling, he could sense it in the air—a blood lust weirdly coinciding with the frenzied eating and shopping seasons of Thanksgiving and Christmas. At this time of year, he did not much care for his neighbors in the valley, nor for the influx of out-of-state hunters, nor, in general, for his fellow man.

"The road bumper-to-bumper with cars, trucks, and four-wheel-drives hours before dawn on opening day!" This is how he always described it, exaggerating for effect at parties.

"The thing is, *we're* the outsiders," his wife Kathleen might sometimes say as they drove the fifteen miles from town to their farmhouse in the western reaches of the Catskill Mountains. "We're the ones who don't fit in. Maybe we should have bought a place in town. We still can, if you think it might be better."

Yes and no. He needed the distancing, the psychological buffer. He, Dieter Jahnke, pianist as well as conductor and musical director of a noted regional orchestra, was a finely tuned mechanism that went delicately awry after too many hours of social interaction, traffic, buildings, the human world at large. A fizz would get into his brain, he'd say, a *fermenting*, that neither aspirin nor sleep could halt for hours afterward. Then, he was capable of little real work until that long, white room within him settled and quieted, the fragmented images and babble and cigarette smoke finally purged. But apart from need, he loved their old house for its own sake—a classic colonial with gabled roof, pilasters, and elegant cornices—a house they had restored at great expense of time and money. Work done not out of love for ostentation, he felt, but rather respect for the house itself and for its first builders and craftsmen, who'd taken such care in a virtual wilderness shortly after the War of 1812.

And, too, there was the land. The narrow valley with its wooded mountains spectacular in every season but particularly in spring, with blossoming shadblow and wild cherry and an array of color as varied as in autumn, if softer. And the good air, the ever-changing clouds, the light. The deer coming to the fields to graze at dusk. The storms, the quiet, the late-spring nights boistrous with peepers and returning geese. Dieter Jahnke, fifty-five years old and a naturalized American citizen who'd lived his early life in a drab East German town, loved it all and loved it deeply. How could it not, he felt, lead him to compose, one day, something quintessentially American, something striking the heart with the same exultant force as Dvořák's *New World Symphony*.

Kathleen, too, found the house and countryside ideal, and whenever she could, spent hours out on location with her watercolors. She was a serene woman generally, fifteen years younger than her husband, but this calm abandoned her each fall, with the advent of archery season in October, and she wasn't really herself, she believed, until the end of muzzle-loading season in December. "It's awful," she'd say, "to find yourself actually dreading this time of year."

"The dying time," as she called it, here once again, she carried a stack of signed, tangerine-colored *No Hunting* signs; he, the heavy-duty stapler as they went out into the cold drizzle. He was wearing his "mad bomber" hat with fake-fur flaps she'd gotten him. A thin man whose face showed hollows that would deepen in time, he always appeared exotically right in formal clothing, his long, graying hair and regal forehead, the dark eyes and finely sculpted nose evocative of some former age's ideal of masculinity, but in a mishmash of sports-clothes, there was something alarming about him, something more on the order of a drug-nourished robber of convenience stores.

They walked an old fence line on the west side of their seventy acres, putting up new *No Hunting* signs and refastening those that had fallen or been pulled down. Near one fallen sign he picked up an aluminum beer can blown by gunfire into a ragged starburst. Like a seismograph, his hand sensed the power of the shell that had done it.

"Careful," she said, "of your hands."

Before they'd bought the property eight years earlier, the house had been vacant for a long time—neighbors and their hunting buddies having free run of its overgrown fields and woods. The Jahnkes' first autumn there, several neighbors had come to the house, politely asking permission to hunt the land. Politely, Dieter had refused permission. Then he began discovering "blinds" and tree stands—platforms built into the lower branches of a tree—all over the place. And arrows, their razor points sunk in earth or lying rusted and exposed, waiting to be stepped on by man or beast. He hired neighbor boys to tear down the stands and blinds, the irony not escaping him that these boys, or their fathers, had probably built them. Seven years after posting the property, the Jahnkes were still finding arrows and every so often a new tree stand, often with a mess of beer cans and whiskey bottles strewn below. The stands were particularly repugnant to Dieter. "How can it be considered hunting?" he'd rage at parties. "Climbing up there well before dawn and just waiting for deer to walk by. How in heaven's name can that be considered *sport?*" After his purge, though, hunters merely drew back to the periphery of the Jahnke property, building their stands inches from the property line but still overlooking the fields. One stand, an elaborate aqua monstrosity mounted ten feet up on a crisscrossing of heavy scaffolding pipe, also painted aqua, looked like what it was, a gun turret, its enclosed, stubby "nest" complete with two plastic windows pushed aside at the bottom to allow firing room. Below, empty beer cans lay all about like metallic droppings. Though he would never admit it to Kathleen, he found this blind quite frightening—the solidity and relative permanence of it, the two eyes giving on his field.

Now, climbing fallen stone walls and stepping over broken barbed-wire fencing, he was angry at himself for not having hired someone to gather up all the old barbed wire and haul it away. He hated seeing a rusted strand of it running through the center of a tree, the tree having encompassed it over time, and its bark there lumpy as scar tissue. He didn't like pounding nails into trees, or even heavy-duty staples. He was either right about all this, he often reflected, or else a disgrace to the male half of the species. But he'd had enough of barbed wire in East Germany and Berlin, having been smuggled into the western sector when he was sixteen, largely at the urging of a piano teacher who'd told his father she could do no more for the boy. His parents had five other children at home, but his mother wept on that last day—the day young Dieter entered the free world, he would say later, in a truckload of muddy potatoes. He supposed his aversion to barbed wire was by now encoded somewhere within those genes floating on their infinitesimal rafts in the vast interior reaches of him. Gun turrets, too.

"D," Kathleen said, stopping. They'd come to their farthest field, where they sometimes went to watch the sun set. The field's centerpiece, a two-hundred-year-old oak, lay toppled like some great branch of coral, its brown leaves stiff and crumpled but still attached. The oak had been cut, they realized, with a chain saw. Someone had taken wood from a few limbs wide as ordinary trees, but the massive trunk lay as it had fallen, solid heartwood exposed, finally, to the weather. From this tree several years earlier, Dieter had removed a blind large enough for two or three men.

Kathleen was able to speak first. It must have happened, she said, while they were in the city the month before. Otherwise she would have heard the noise. Unless she'd been in town. "Do they actually know my *schedule,* whoever did it? Is it possible they just wanted some firewood?"

"No," he said.

The limbs were speckled with tan gypsy-moth egg masses, but the oak had recovered from three seasons of gypsy-moth infestation. What it had not recovered from, Dieter thought, was *him.*

"I will call the sheriff." His stomach churned. His brain went into its boiling-over fizz. This he himself had done. He'd done this. What they wanted was revenge. He dared not say it, hardly dared think it.

"Kathe," he said. "I do not think you should be coming out here alone, painting."

"But it's our *land*. I won't be intimidated! Bad enough we have to stay cooped up and can't walk anywhere during all these stupid hunting seasons! My God—they start in October, the bow hunters, and then it doesn't end until—when? It's crazy!"

Move, he thought. Start over. Why not in town—somewhere on the fringes, woodsy but not the frontier. Or in the town itself. Someplace with a nice garden behind old wrought-iron fencing. But it seemed he hadn't the energy to walk back and get on with the day, now, never mind uprooting and moving elsewhere. They should have a gun. Oh, he wished he had one. He in his mad bomber hat, following the men hauling chain saws and gas cans on their all-terrain vehicles. Stalking them, and they not hearing a thing in all the racket they liked to surround themselves with, and then, when they stopped their engines, he would step out into the quiet clearing and say, "Good afternoon, gentlemen—" Oh, it would be so good to do. His long fingers trembled with the need to be doing that just then. But there would be the next day and the next, and while he rehearsed with the orchestra, other trees would crash down.

He stapled a *No Hunting* sign to the oak's horizontal trunk. It was getting colder, the light sinking. He sensed, crazily, hunters watching them, having waited for this moment. He turned to the woods, where shadows made a heavy line under a fringe of hemlocks, their tops lost in fog. He waved the stapler. "See you boys tomorrow!" Kathleen looked at him in alarm.

Walking back through the woods, halfway to the house, it was his turn to stop abruptly.

"What is it?" she said.

Ahead on the trail were the remains of a deer, a recent kill, its head and hindquarters gone, the rest left for turkey buzzards and foxes— and probably for them as well. To see.

"Our poacher," he said. "Or else arrow hunters." The poacher was a neighbor who kept two freezers in a truck-body garage, both heaped, Dieter had reason to believe, with illegal venison the man sold to friends and possibly to an expensive new restaurant in town advertising wild game entrées.

"Should we get the camera?" she said.

"It is too dark. We can come here tomorrow."

"Tomorrow's opening day."

"We need better light. Let's go back." He wanted to go home now—their daughter alone in the house.

Kathleen said, "I'm thinking we should have a gun. What's the difference between a shotgun and a rifle, do you know, D?"

He didn't. He knew nothing about guns, nor about how to use them. And at the moment, it seemed, he knew nothing at all.

All that day there'd been a holiday quiet over their dirt road, no traffic at all, but in the fog and damp it seemed ominous, and now that night had fallen, men were out in their vehicles, not tearing by as they did on Saturday nights, but cruising at walking speed, which Dieter found more threatening. The sound of rumbling engines, a mounted spotlight's beam scanning fields, woods, their house, and taking so long in its probing passage. Spotlighting deer, it was called. Trying to find out where they were—for the next day. Jacking deer was when they shot them after dark, the deer immobilized by the light. He'd seen a TV program about a woman and her husband somewhere out west who'd taken off in their truck after spotlighters. The husband wound up shot dead, dying in her arms, and the bereaved woman lost her court case against the killer. That's the kind of fool he was, he thought, to think he could scare *them*.

He closed the dining-room drapes, and they sat down to a candle-light meal celebrating their daughter Erica's first weekend home from college. They bowed their heads before beginning, and Dieter prayed in silence for their safety. *Take me, if You wish. Take me instead.* He touched his chest, trying to calm a heart tapping arhythmically at this prospect. One day it would happen. His patient dark angel coming to light. But he'd done quite a bit of decent work in his lifetime, and perhaps his best was behind him. Possibly he was deluding himself with thoughts of some great new work still ahead. He looked at his daughter, the long, pale forehead his, but the mass of sienna hair Kathleen's. That he'd done, he and Kathleen—a great thing. Why must he demand more, always more? Then he was hearing Schubert's Impromptu in A-flat Major, played by Alfred Brendel. Kathleen had put it on, he knew, to cheer him up.

"D," she said, "aren't you hungry?"

"I am! But we should have a toast, don't you think?"

"A toast!"

They raised their goblets, but Dieter noticed, high on the wall behind his wife, the chandelier's branching shadow, and there it was again—the savage cut through perfect wood.

"Daddy, are you really going to do your thing tomorrow?"

"My thing? And what is that?"

"You know!"

"Oh! Yes, I will do it. I vow to do it. The alarm's already set. They would miss it otherwise. It is the performance of the year out here."

"I don't believe you guys. They probably think you're totally gonzo, you and mom."

"I'm sure they think along those lines, that's true."

"I have a tape you can borrow."

"What is it?"

"Trust me. They'll love it."

"Is it, as they say, heavy?"

"Very."

"Is it, like, jangly and bangly?"

"Worse than that."

"Terribly bad, then."

"Totally bad. You have to say it right."

"Bad. Totally."

"Wicked bad."

"Now there's a word."

"Awesome!"

"Awesome and terrible and totally negligent and careless of the eardrums."

"That's it, *totally*," she said, and laughed, his daughter.

He couldn't sleep. He kept hearing engines, kept imagining
the probe of light sliding over fields, illuminating trees, clapboard,

windows—looking, looking—then lingering for a while on the suddenly revealed form of a deer, its eyes stars, then moving on, the probe—searching, searching some more. At two he got up and went into the bathroom where he had laid out his clothes. At three Kathleen found him in the kitchen, dressed and ready to go.

"It's too early," she said. "We have at least two hours yet. You'll be exhausted by the afternoon."

"I cannot sleep." The first rifle-hunting season they'd experienced, living in the house, he'd been startled awake by a barrage of gunfire on opening day, everywhere on their property, it'd seemed, and some of it sounding like dynamite blasting. "What is it?" he'd cried out, a little boy in an East German *strasse*. Since that time, he always awoke before the firing began.

"I think," Kathleen said now, "we must be out of our minds. What do you think?"

"That we are not free to do otherwise."

"Oh, but we are. We can sell. Move. It might be better than having you killed. That tree—it was a warning."

"Who will kill me? What American in his right mind wishes to go to prison."

"An *accident*," she said. "It would be so easy. To stage."

"*Ja*," he said. "Then let them stage. We will see."

Flashlight. Blaze orange hat. Blaze orange vest over his jacket. Tape deck. Tape. Camera. Gloves. Notebook. Pencil. Portable phone—with which to call Kathleen, and she the conservation officer or the conservation officer's wife or the county sheriff. Dieter was ready.

There was an inch of fresh snow on the ground, with more falling. This was bad because it was good for them—the hunters. But it was also good for Dieter. Now he could track the hunters, if need be. Now he could follow them right to their nests or blinds or whatever it was they called their cunning devices. Hoo, Dieter, watch yourself now! Here we go!

On went the tape deck at the west property line, his daughter's tape—pounding electronic noise wonderfully confused, yet form managing to emerge here and there. Did she take it seriously? he wondered. Did she really like it? Still, it did have something. Heartbeat and racing pulse. Improvisation that flew right to the edge. Dared to—as he might today. His own racing pulse amazed him, the manic high. Could it be this was something of what it was all about—hunting? He shone his flashlight into overgrown fields. "Wake up! Wake up!" he called into the dark. "They are coming soon! They'll be here. Wake up! Run now! It's time. It's time." He hoped to chase any deer toward the center of the property but knew they might overrun it and keep going. Still, running was better than standing still.

And then movement in the dark, sensed. He turned down the tape, aimed the flashlight, and heard some frantic crashing through undergrowth. A large buck plunged out of the woods, leaping the stone wall and passing so close, swerving to avoid him, that Dieter could clearly see his white muzzle and imagined himself reflected in those large eyes knowing only fear—fleeing Dieter's sanctuary. The animal exuded some magnetic field of terror that drew Dieter into its whirlpool, and for a while he could only stand there, shaken, until he saw the tracks. Two persons walking side by side in the direction the deer had come from. Anger made him suddenly fearless. "My good people," he hollered, "if you are here, you should not be! Leave at once or I shall find you and report you." He heard a quiet sifting of snow against dry leaves and angled the flashlight upward, revealing old beech leaves clinging to silver-gray limbs. Snow fell like particles of light through the foggy column. "Be assured," he called, "I too am armed!" He turned up the heavy-metal tape and followed the tracks.

They led to the fallen oak—its web of dark branches outlined in a complexity of white. He could see where the two had stood for a while, probably with their own flashlights, taking in tree and posted notice. "I am coming!" he said. "I am right behind you, still!" A fit of trembling possessed him—legs, arms, the hand holding the tape player shaking as if he were freezing. They were just ahead, he thought, or just to the side, concealed in their nest and watching him approach. But, no. The tracks led on. "Hoo-oo!" he hollered into the noise of the music and laughing to himself at what he must sound—and look—like. "You are on private land here and must leave at once!"

At that he expected to hear a shot, the bullet whizzing by his ear, as in cowboy movies, but there was nothing except the nerve-scouring music. He turned off the tape and called Kathleen at the house.

"Get the Stankavage fellow," he said, his mouth, numbing with cold, having difficulty with the words. "Someone is here."

"Hunters, you mean?"

"*Ja,* they are here, somewhere. Tell him to meet me halfway down the east line."

The conservation officer was not on his side, Dieter knew, because he was a city-folk pest, especially at Stankavage's busiest times, and a foreigner on top of it all. The man, a retired electrician and unfailingly low-keyed, let him know this without having to say a word. The night before, he'd promised—hollowly, Dieter thought—to see to the matter of the slain deer. "I'll look into it, Mr. Jan-ky. I have my eye on some folks. I can't say nothin' about it now, but I have my eye on 'em." Dieter suspected that he was either afraid of the poacher or else in on it with him. Police dogs had tracked the scent of a kill straight to the two freezers in the fluorescent-lit, truck-body garage where hundreds of pounds of venison were found, but the poacher had gotten off with only a warning.

"Dieter," Kathleen said, "come back. "I've been thinking . . . This really is insane. Your life means more to me than this house, property, and all the deer on it. I want you to come back."

"Kathe, Kathe," he said. "I will. Soon. It is now a point of honor!"

It wasn't, but he felt giddy and exhilarated and afraid in the thinning dark, and the foolish words just came.

One shot, then another, then several somewhere nearby. Dieter stood still on his small island of quiet. Not even dawn yet, not completely, and the shooting already begun.

"Hello!" he called out. "If you are still here, you are on private lands and must go. There will be no hunting here, my good people!"

The music on once again, he continued tracking the two, his heart hurting with the climb, the exertion, the fear, his face stinging with cold, his breath coming short and frosted. The tracks stopped at a high outcropping of fissured rock along a ridge, the rock's crevices ample enough to conceal man or animal.

"Hide and seek," Dieter called, "is a game for children. Reveal yourself at once, for I know you are right there!" In that instant, Dieter understood the appeal of the Rambo movies, Terminator movies. The power, the gloating, self-righteous need—yes!—to pull the trigger and be done with evil forever. Rub them out! Take them out! Waste them!

A plump man, his face deep pink, emerged, his rifle lowered, his head as well. Then came a thin boy with his own gun. The boy looked no older than Erica, Dieter thought, and might even be younger. The man stood out, pumpkin-like, in his blaze orange, but the boy, in camouflage jacket and dark Levi's, appeared nearly invisible against the moss and lichen-covered rock. This fellow wasn't, Dieter knew, the poacher, a bony, virile man. This was somebody else—someone he felt sure he'd once met.

"We're sorry," the man began. "We thought we was off your land. We just cut across."

The old story! We thought this, we thought that. We didn't see no signs! But Dieter's heart was easing its strained rush, and his legs seemed able, once again, to hold him. The woods, the rock, the man, and the boy seemed to reverberate before him, too vivid, but it all meant that he was alive. Still. These fellows could have shot him any-time, but no, here he was. Heat seeped upward, scorching his face.

"I believe I've met you before," he said, "haven't I?"

"Yes sir. I work at Blum's and delivered your waterbed, Mr. Janky. This here's my boy. His first year out. We apologize being on your property."

"Ah," Dieter said, his hands now, too, burning up, and his ears. "Well, you are. It's just, we do not want—the killing here."

"I understand that, Mr. Janky. I do. We'll be goin', then."

"I am sorry as well." He did feel sorrow, then—for the three of them, the embarrassment, the whole thing maybe spoiled for the boy. But these were crazy thoughts, Dieter knew. It should be spoiled for the boy. He should not be taught to be a killer! *Get their numbers.*

But he didn't. He let them go, watching their diminishing shapes against white as they moved toward woods beyond his land. He waited, then followed at a distance, still playing the tape, though not as loudly.

"You walk around with that music blaring, D, and you don't even hear the shooting," Kathleen said when he returned at mid-morning to warm himself in the kitchen and have a cup of coffee. "You could get shot yourself, honestly. You could walk right into gunfire and not know it!" They went through this each year, Dieter always arguing that as a landowner in America, a land of freedom, he was free to have no blood spilled on his land, if he so wished. He respected—more or less—others' right to slaughter creatures left and right and fatten the coffers of the so-called Department of Environmental Conservation in the process, but they must correspondingly respect his right to keep his land free of such barbarisms. The sophisticated, high-powered weapons! The blinds and nests! Yet he wasn't thinking so much, now, about these things but rather about how he'd avoided the aqua blind that morning, its two blank eyes, the men no doubt there, drinking probably, while they waited—for him.

"Stankavage did not come," he said.

"Then he probably didn't get the message from his wife."

"I will buy him, for Christmas, a car telephone."

"I'm sure he'll thank you for that."

"Listen to them. Worse this year. It is like war. What they must hear on the streets of Beirut. *Why?*"

"They say it's how they keep in touch with nature."

"*Ja.* A good joke."

"D? I don't want you going out there again. You've done enough. I'm putting my foot down, and I mean it."

He looked at her foot in its tapestry slipper against the wide floor-boards. Pretty! His beauty, his Kathleen—who'd made everything so nice, the gardens, the lawn, renewing, restoring, pulling it all from weedy oblivion, working so hard.

"I do think we should consider moving," she was saying. "Maybe wait until we're calmer and discuss it. I really hate having to say so, but to be under seige like this for weeks on end is really too awful. I can work in town, just the same. So can you, D. We should be rational about it."

But now he did not want to be rational. He did not want to surrender. Neither to them nor to his own fears. Get run off the land! No, no. He must be Gary Cooper, John Wayne, Randolph Scott. He must run them off and keep them off. After all, this was America, land of the free.

"You're too quiet," she said. "I know what you're thinking."

"I will be good," he said, "and you must be careful, driving."

She had to go into town to teach her museum class and would take Erica with her. They would have to wear blaze orange vests and caps while driving. And even that was no guarantee of safety, but—irony of ironies—they would look like hunters! Oh, she was right. It was foolish to stay when everything cut across the grain as it did.

"Promise me you won't go out there again when I'm gone," she said. "I'm too young to be a widow."

"I will be good, I assure you!"

"That's not a promise."

"I will, then, cross my heart."

When they had left, Dieter sat down at his piano and played Beethoven sonatas, Scarlatti sonatas, then Ives and Copland, Schubert and Mozart. He went back to the Copland, the Ives. He played Scott Joplin rags and a Gershwin concert waltz, hoping to see through the music into— Something. What he'd only glimpsed, somehow, in the woods. That deer, then the plump fellow and his boy—in such get-ups. And how bad he'd felt, chasing them away. He lifted his hands from the piano, then sat with them in his lap. In the waning light, vehicles were again moving slowly by. Road hunters, they were disparagingly called, scanning yards and posted fields near houses, their heads swiveling from side to side. He remembered Kathleen's words, her concern and his promise, and for a while tried to cultivate quietude. He paged through a book on American architecture, then walked from room to room, turning on lamps. From long windows, he watched vehicles passing, hunters intent, on the alert. When a pickup came by slowly, filled in back with armed men, their red and orange colors glowing against a backdrop of pale blue snow, anger and mad energy again claimed him, and he rushed to put on his own blaze orange. At sunset—a thin wash of coral light against heavy cloud cover—he walked up his hillside, banging a wooden spoon against a skillet and singing German folk songs while gunfire in every direction came like staccato pops from some out-of-sync percussion section hitting against his heart.

When he returned, intact but exhausted, he saw, in the lights from the house, that someone had thrown a bag of garbage on the front lawn. He went to get it and put it in the barn, but it was open, its steaming contents spilling out over the grass. "Oh, it is too much," he said to the night. "My good people, this is too much."

Half an hour later, in blaze orange and mad bomber hat, he carried the bag into the Liberty Inn, where, outside, nine bucks hung from a beam lashed to trees, and the parking lot was filled with pickups and four-wheel-drives.

"Maestro!" someone called. People at tables looked up. Men and women at the bar turned.

"Gentlemen," he announced to the room, "I bring you your trophy, which was inadvertently left on my lawn." He placed the bag on the floor and untied it.

"Oh, my God," a woman at a nearby table said, as the bag fell on its side and some of its contents slid out. "That's *gross.*"

"Buy the maestro a beer!" someone called. "Looks like he's had a tough day."

"Get your buck?" someone else hollered.

Young men in orange and camouflage were grinning. Young women turned to watch him. A space at the bar opened, the bartender placing a glass of draft there.

"Have a drink, maestro, on the house!" a man at the bar said. "Take a load off." A woman laughed. The band members, in turquoise shirts, string ties, and black and white hide vests, walked toward their instruments on the platform behind a small dance floor. Dieter was not trembling as much now and made a good show of walking forward with boldness. He raised the beer glass and drank it all.

"Lookit the man *chug* it! Get 'im another!"

"No," Dieter said. "Thank you."

The bartender, Les, slid a quart jar full of dollars and fives toward him. "Care to contribute?"

He'd been about to leave, having made his point—whatever it was—but he stopped. "What is it for?"

Les named a family, explaining that the man had taken his own life that day in the woods after discovering he'd killed his boy, mistaking him for a deer. "They was out your way for a while," he said. "Earlier.

That's what I hear, anyway." The bartender looked down at the jar of
money. Men and women on either side of them seemed to stiffen,
withdrawing into silence. Elsewhere in the room, laughter and talk
and rock-a-billy music, but it receded, and the plump man was standing in front of the outcropping with his boy, saying *I can understand
that. We didn't know—* When Dieter opened his eyes, a shot of whiskey awaited him on the bar. He drank it all, at once, then put what
money he had with him into the quart jar. Before leaving, he wrote
down the widow's name.

Outside, he placed the bag of viscera under the hanging deer strung
up from the neck. He looked at the deer for a long time—their racks,
the heads lopped over, the stick-like forelegs turning slightly in each
gust of wind, flakes of snow glittering on fur. Then he wiped his
hands and went back into the bar. Standing in the doorway, he looked
at the roomful of people. Slowly, noise and music burned away. He
did not see that the faces turned toward him were unsmiling now, and
anxious, but only felt the hush of an audience waiting for him to raise
the baton and begin. A man coming into the bar stopped when the
bartender called, "Get outta here! Get back outside!"

These words jarred Dieter. Were they actually afraid—of him? "Oh,
my good people," he said. "Do not be frightened, not of me. I only
wish to say how terrible it is, what today happened. Think what he
must have seen, that poor fellow, to what depth he must have traveled
in a single awful instant." Dieter waved his right arm. "Oh, terrible.
But to see, to finally see—!"

The crowd was staring at him through a haze of cigarette smoke
wavering as if they were all underwater, creatures alien to one another.
The room seemed to darken further, and he sensed someone in the
back raising a gun, taking aim at him. Covering his face, he felt the
stickiness of his hands and smelled the pungent odor of butcher shops,
where organ meats lay bloody in their white enamel trays. He waited,
knowing it would come—out of such vast indifference it had to—but
there was no sudden gunfire, no movement, and after a while he lowered his hands. Men standing near the pool table were holding only
cue sticks; the band, its instruments; people at the bar and tables, their
drinks and cigarettes. Then Dieter saw a child among them, a boy of
about five or six, wearing a blaze-orange vest over his jacket. He was
seated between a young couple at a table bordering the dance floor,

his face, turned to Dieter Jahnke, flushed and scared and still.

"Oh my good people! Just look!" He pointed to the child. "*Look.* Oh please. Let us—"

His throat tightened. Preaching! Up on some soapbox! Don't do as I do, do as I say. "Forgive me," he said finally, "this interruption. But it was too much, today. Today was too much." He bowed, as if from his podium, and then the bartender was there, a hand on his shoulder, gently escorting him outside.

The bartender's thick flannel shirt was rolled to the elbows and he wore no coat but seemed unaffected by the cold wind. On his broad forearm, nearly obscured by still-black hair, was a blue anchor and snaky rope. "You want me to call your wife for you? I can call her if you want."

There were tears in Dieter Jahnke's eyes, and he let them come. "She is not home," he was able to say. "No one is home yet. None of us!" Throwing open his arms, he embraced the startled bartender, gripping him hard and pounding him on the back. "But you are a good fellow, and I thank you."

He drove slowly, headlights probing the night, eyes straining to see into the woods on either side. Above all now, he did not want to hit a deer—they'd still be running, still panicky. But instead, he saw those hanging from the crossbeam, saw the plump man apologizing, and he himself saying, *No, no, stay here, you can hunt, you have my permission,* but the two of them going away through the woods, and then the man cut straight through with grief, split with the shock of it, and life sliding out, brilliant and silken, becoming earth, wind, nothing, becoming some rushing dark music leaping up before him now with the wild careening motion of creatures on the run.

Kathleen and Erica found him there later that night, the car pulled over onto the narrow shoulder, its engine off, the headlights and interior lights on but dim, the glove compartment rifled of all its paper scraps. Dieter looked up from his notations, startled to find his wife opening the door, her face chalky.

"My God, D, we thought—"

"Oh no, no. I am all right. But I had to—"

"Thank God. When we saw the *car*—"

"No, no, I am all right, but I see I have drained the battery."

Kathleen drove her car and he sat in the back, wondering how to make it up to her, to them both for the bad scare, for what he would have to tell them soon, yet here they were, here they were again, oh, a gift, a gift, and who deserved? Holding the scraps of paper and owner's manual scribbled over with his terrifying new work, he watched the road, the shoulders of the road, the woods, the dark, and felt it pulsing through him—that fierce good thing all but cleaving open the heart.

DINOSAURS

"You're *kidding*," Anita said.

"No, I swear to God," Tommy V. told her. "The guy just needed to make his car payments."

"How big did you say?"

"Twenty *acres*."

"*Un*-believable. I was thinking maybe a miniature golf-type place, or something."

"No! Acres! The guy must be nuts. Why don't you come up there with me, you and Billy?"

"To see it?"

"Sure, see it. Stay, if you want. I bet we could make a go of it, you and me."

Her hand curved around his beer glass, the fingernails little red hearts. Then she whisked it away, black skirt, white blouse, all business.

He couldn't believe he said that—*make a go of it, you and me.* The dumb way it sounded, and how she'd probably take it the wrong way. Would she bring the refill or ignore him? Ignore, he figured. Keep away, waiting for him to leave. But the thing was, they *could* make a go of the place, maybe. She was a hard worker, and he had the property, and the property had lots of potential. And he'd always believed you got out of life what you put into it—a fact that usually depressed him when he thought about it, because the other side of the coin was, you had to put your energy and willpower into the *right* thing. And this is where he always screwed up. Royally. He'd known guys who went to school on the G.I. Bill, learned meat-cutting or TV repairing or what have you and then started their own businesses and now were sitting pretty. Nice big houses. Families. Grandkids. No money worries. As for him, he'd fallen into and out of hourly-wage jobs, never his own boss, never the right thing; into and out of a marriage and nothing to show for it except regret, bad feelings, and two sons living near their mother in Texas. Then a little too much drinking over the years, an accident in a fork-lift factory, and now his bum hip pinned together, early retirement and peanuts pension. Retirement. Sometimes this struck him as funny, other times as grounds for suicide. What got him was how you're young for a hell of a long time and it seems there's always something ahead of you somewhere, something you'll find or will find you, but then one day you know, you just *know* you're old and the whole shooting match is over. You don't even have to look at the bunchy, old-man skin, the color leaking away, you just wake up one day and it's there, inside you, *Hey, Tommy!* and you wind up carrying that around with you too, bad as those pins in your hip.

But now the pins were drumming a crazy new message. *Anita.* Even though she liked to kid around at the bar, saying she was over the hill too, she wasn't. Not in his book. She was only in her early fifties, whereas he was pushing sixty-five. On her good days, she looked maybe thirty-five, with her figure and hair and pep. The pep was the main thing. When her only son and daughter-in-law were killed by a drunk driver, she took in her grandson, an infant, and people who didn't know the story assumed Billy was her own child. "You can't let it get to you, kiddo," she liked to say, "or you're dead in the water." Recently, when the boy's junior high became caught up in a gang thing—kids beating up on other kids and stealing lunch money, she gave a speech at a P.T.A. meeting and was quoted in the newspaper. Reporters now stopped at the bar and wrote her words down in notebooks and called her Anita. She laughed with them, flirting. She had sunken half-circles under her eyes, but the rest of her skin was shiny and moist—a lot of makeup, but so what? It looked good. Her short blond hair sprang away from the terry cloth headbands she wore, and he didn't mind the black roots at times. Then her hair reminded him of some bright shrub flaring up from strong dark stems. He'd never gotten up the courage to ask her out. He figured seeing her here, at the bar, was all the out a guy in his position could reasonably expect, and be glad for the laughs and small talk, the friendly routine of it. So why the heck did he have to blow it with his madman *make a go of it, you and me.*

"Were you serious, Tommy?"

There was his refill, and the little hearts. "Sure."

"You think it could fly?"

The pins throbbed. "I don't see why not. I keep hearing there's nothing like it up there. Except, maybe, for this place that's got the World's Largest Cross."

"Where's that? Close by?"

"Thirty miles or so, but no big deal. Could be a tie-in, I'm thinking. You know. A tour bus, or tourists in cars, could stop there and then at the Dinosaur Gardens, or vice versa."

She kept her head down. "I don't believe this."

He didn't, either.

"Tommy, I don't have any money to sink into it. I mean big bucks."

"That's OK. It's paid for. I can swing the rest."

"Also, I'm talking a business thing. I mean strictly. You know?" Her brown eyes flicked away and back, then away again.

"Sure," he said.

"The thing is, all the drugs here, in the schools and everywhere— I'm sick of it."

"Yeah, right. Hard to raise kids."

"So," she said, giving him the benefit of those brown eyes, "I'm thinking, what the hell. Let's."

"Oh God," Anita said, getting out of the car after their day-long drive north from Detroit. "I'm too old for this!" Her Celebrity rode low on its springs, loaded on top with ladders and, inside, with all their luggage and supplies. Tommy couldn't walk at first and had

to stand there on the weedy gravel, hunched forward a little and pretending to size up the scene—two log cabins, their white chinking and
corner logs alone defining them against dark woods. Billy kept close to
Anita. Tommy felt sorry for him and liked him well enough but
wished, now, that things were a little different. The cabins looked
small as hell. The pins in his hip were sending out all kinds of angry
and scared messages which he interpreted mainly as Dumb! Stupid!
Look at this place. There wasn't even a sign saying Dinosaur Gardens.
He did not believe, then, there were any dinosaurs here. The pins were
telling him what he already knew. The guy had pulled a fast one, and
he, Tommy V., was an A-number-one jerk for getting sucked in. Again.

She was too polite to say anything, he sensed, so he had to. "Well,"
he said. "This is it. Custer's last stand."

"The thing is," Anita would say, "we just have to keep our spirits
up. Not *defeat* ourselves right off the bat." And she had kept their
spirits up, right from that first night, fixing a little party for them of
pop and beer and salami sandwiches and the "homemade" brownies
they'd bought at a gas station and convenience store just off the Inter-
state. But the cottage was damp, and Tommy's hip ached hard that
first night. The light bulb in the ceiling fixture might have been a
floodlight, and held within it, Anita looked her age. Worse. He
couldn't shake fear, not even the next morning when they all stepped
outside to a wet, green world so lush and sweet-smelling it seemed
edible—a world of pine and cedar and fern and wet sandy soil, a world
disturbed only by the enthusiasm of many birds and a few cars zinging
by on the two-lane highway.

Everywhere they looked, though, was work. Big-project work. The
other cabin proved to be a wreck of a snack bar and souvenir shop,
now a cluttered storeroom of damp cardboard boxes and long shelves
messy with scattered key chains, postcards, educational toys, and tiny
plastic dinosaurs strewn everywhere. But they gave Tommy hope. If
these, then somewhere, maybe, the big ones, the real thing.

And then they found them—back in the cedar swamp. Massive
concrete shapes lurking just off overgrown, muddy paths. Paint flaking off. Teeth hanging loose. Eyes blurry with fading paint. Armored
plates broken off. Tails. Blood spots turning pink. Several appeared to
be sinking in some tropical rain forest. One, a great bird-like creature,

was stuck in a clump of low cedar growth, flopped there all askew and gazing at them with an outraged eye.

"That's a pterodactyl," Billy said.

"A what?" Tommy turned to the boy. "How d'you know that!"

"He knows them all!" Anita said. "I meant to tell you. Kids are *into* dinosaurs today!"

Flushed with praise, Billy ran ahead of them on the path, jumping streamlets of boggy water where footbridges had rotted and fallen apart. In a pond all black water and chartreuse algae, an elephant-like creature made its last stand against three life-sized human figures in loincloths who aimed long poles, their sharpened tips pink with faded paint.

"*Un*-believable!"

Anita repeated the word when they came upon a giant concrete snake, erect and appearing to watch them at eye level. "Most women," she said, "would be outta here by now. Hi, sweetheart! How ya doin?" She patted the snake's chipped, black head. "Benches, we need. Also, to fix those bridges. And," she raised a wet, blackened sneaker, "something for the paths, sawdust or something. So people don't get all mucky. Darn it, we need a notebook."

And Tommy was saying to himself, benches, bridges, paths. This I can do. I can *do* this.

A rickety wrought-iron stairway led to a doorway in the last display, a dinosaur whose tree-like legs lifted him high into the cedar and poplar and balsam. His long neck curved away into the swamp. So did his tail. They all wanted to see what was inside and decided to go one at a time, Tommy first, in case—as Anita said—"there might be something not nice, if you know what I mean."

But inside the dinosaur's belly was a plain room with a small window looking out on tree branches, and another smaller window set into a partition across the dinosaur's chest area. Through it a tiny room was just visible, empty except for a picture of Christ with a warped sign underneath. *The Greatest Heart in the World.*

"That's got to go!" Anita said, clumping down the stairs. "Now *that* is creepy."

Tommy thought it was interesting in some oddball way, and something they might be able to tie in with the Greatest Cross thing, but

Anita wanted nothing to do with the idea. It was "freaky," they'd be called religious freakos, and people would stay away in droves. Besides, the steps were too dangerous, and they couldn't afford high insurance premiums. Deciding to leave well enough alone, Tommy pulled away the stairs so no one would be tempted.

"Listen," she said, reading his bleak look. "Everybody starts small. *Everybody* has to overcome obstacles in the beginning. You can't let it get to you!"

Other words had gotten into his head, though, and wouldn't leave. *Sixty-four, another door! Sixty-four, another door!*

"Let's shoot for the Fourth of July," she said. "A grand opening."

That was only a few weeks away. The pins were pulsing in protest. "There's a heck of a lot of work."

"So? We just knuckle down and *do* it."

But while he and Billy got to work, first cleaning the cabins, then painting, then clearing spaces around the dinosaurs, Anita fooled around—that's how Tommy put it to himself though he was careful not to say anything. He figured she needed to scout around, check out the territory, meaning the town fourteen miles away. She called this her public relations campaign—talking the place up, making contacts, sending out the word. Probably a good idea, he thought, but the place was too quiet without her. Just a watery wind in the cedars and poplars, the streams burbling away, and every now and then a mosquito honing in on its target. Once in a while there'd be a car or a semi in the distance, and then the arcing roar as it sped by, and then just leaves and wind again. When she returned around five with food, treats, and stories about finding a good beauty shop or grocery or running into "this neat guy" from the Chamber of Commerce or the Kiwanis, it was party time again, and he'd tell himself that he worried too much. Brooded. Always. And it had to stop. He remembered the words of an athlete he'd read about in a newspaper article—"Give up on yourself and the door closes."

"So what did *you* guys do today?" Anita would ask finally, winding down. Tommy would look at Billy and Billy would get his vague, scared look, so Tommy would start it off. Fixed this footbridge. Hauled wood chips and shredded bark up to this or that point.

Painted Sam or Jake or Verna—his names for the dinosaurs, whose real names were, he felt, totally beyond him.

"And how about you, honey?" she'd say to Billy.

"Helped."

"He's a darn good worker, too," Tommy might add, not wanting the silence.

"You miss your friends?"

"They weren't my friends."

"You miss home, then?"

"It's OK here."

And Tommy, exhaling, would turn his attention to Anita's newly colored and set jumble of hair, thinking, Oh Christ, let it be. Just this one time, let it *be*, OK?

Their cottage had two bedrooms, each with a flowered drape for a doorway. The daybed in the main room, near a squat cast-iron stove, was Billy's, and Tommy made bookshelves for him and drove in a few nails for clothing. In each bedroom was a chipped iron bedstead with a sagging mattress on buoyant, noisy springs, and a mirrored dresser whose drawers, when opened, emitted a musty, pungent odor. Each night the musical springs in Anita's bedroom sang to his imagination, his hopes—all crazy and impossible, he knew. In the cabin, anyway, where the racket alone might bring down the mossy roof. He counted himself lucky, each morning, when he couldn't remember his dreams.

One afternoon, Anita returned early from town and, holding back the drape to Tommy's bedroom, found him sitting on the edge of his bed. He'd been lying down and hadn't been able to stand quickly enough when he heard her car.

"You OK?"

"Sure," he said. "Just tired."

"It's cold in here. You should be outside in the sun. Where's Billy?"

"In the snack bar. Making signs, or maybe hanging posters."

"I have a terrific *surprise* for you!"

He opened the grocery bag, hoping for strawberry shortcake, or better yet, a six-pack, but pulled out something that turned out to be—though he didn't say so out loud—a Jungle Jim suit. Khaki jacket with big square pockets. Buttons all over hell and back. And those goofy straps or whatever on the shoulders. And pants with big pockets. An outfit he wouldn't be caught dead or alive in.

"Look at those creases!" she said. "It's never been worn."

"I wonder why."

"That's what I wondered too! I found it at this neat thrift shop."

"Do they give refunds?"

"You don't like it?"

"It might be OK—for somebody."

"Try it on."

"It won't fit."

"How do you know! I bet it will. I held it up."

"I don't want to wear this, Anita. It's a gimmick."

Her displeasure pushed into the room. "That's exactly what we'll need! A gimmick! People love gimmicks. Everybody wants some kind of fantasy. You can be the safari *guide!* They'll love it."

"This is a dinosaur place, not some big game park."

"Same difference. Tommy? You have a pretty good build, you know that? You could look nice."

"What do I look like now?"

"Now? Most of the time—like a slob-ola."

She let the drape fall back. Her bedsprings screeched at him. So did the pins holding his hip together. He put on the outfit without looking into the mirror, then gave her a tour of all they'd done that day. New wood chips spread along the paths glowed in the early evening light. The air was fragrant with damp cedar bark.

"*Un*-believable! Oh, this is going to work. I have a good feeling about it! And look at *you*." Words zinging through him, and gold flecks everywhere—on the path, in her hair, on eyelids, arms, chin. "Let's *see*," she said, laughing as she unbuttoned the safari jacket. "Let's just see that nice build of yours!" Desire, then, and panic—Where was the boy!—as she led him, safari jacket flapping in the warm wind, toward a dry couch of wood chips. *This is it, Tommy,* the pins sang afterward.

And it seemed to be, even after a drizzly Fourth of July weekend that drew only a few people—parents propelling their children back to heated cars and campers that sped them somewhere else. Tommy, dressed in his safari outfit, offered his services as guide to a group that'd come in a vacation vehicle as large, it seemed, as one of the cabins. "This one here," he told them, "and you can read his name right there, on that sign—this big fellow could only eat grass and water weeds and such, so you figure it was easy for the other guys to gang up on him. Just like today." At the mammoth under attack, he said, "And here we have man at work, doing what we do, pretty much." At the big snake, "Watch out for this guy! He means business." And at the last footbridge, "My wife over in the snack bar over there is waiting for us with some nice, free hot coffee and some pop for the kids. We can go over there right now, if you want." But they took off for their snazzy vehicle, as Tommy later put it, like bats.

Soon after this, Anita got the idea of making Billy the guide, since he was so good with the names. Besides, it would draw him out and possibly help him, later, in school. "People," she observed, "are noticing your *limp*. And when people feel sorry for somebody, they just want to get away." But she made him wear the outfit anyway. "It looks official. People naturally *respect* uniforms."

Lying on the wood chips and looking up at the canopy of woods—his trees!—he thought how he'd never done such a thing before—lying on the ground, looking up at the sky—except maybe when he was a kid. And now here he was. Earth and sky, sky and earth.

"What're you thinking?" Anita said. "You look pretty darn happy."

"I was thinking I can't believe I own this."

"That's true," she said, sitting up and getting into her red jogging outfit. "That is true."

And he knew he'd blown it.

A few days later, while they were washing dishes in the snack bar where they had their meals, he asked her to marry him. Share the wealth.

"Are you serious?"

She was offering him a way out, he sensed. Everything warned him to make a joke of it, but he said, "Sure, I am."

She covered his hand with her soapy rubber glove and said she needed to think about it. It was a pretty big step for someone like her.

Was it? Why? He thought of his limp and how she'd fired him from being guide because he couldn't say the dinosaurs' real names. He took Billy into town with him one afternoon and came back with a new haircut, a dictionary from the thrift shop, and a notebook from Woolworth's. Nights, the two of them worked on names, while Anita did her nails or tried to watch the snowy TV.

"Wait," he said. "Don't tell me. I know it! The pinhead one."

"They're all pinheads," Anita said, "if you ask me."

"The Stegmeir one!"

"He's thinking of beer," Anita said. "Again."

"A stego-sore ass is what he'd get if he tried to sit down on all them plates."

Billy and Anita regarded him, offended and bored.

"Just a joke! It helps me remember."

In August Anita enrolled Billy in a country school only six miles away but lost interest in their walks to the wood chip pile. The bad canceled out the good, in his book, though he resolved to make the best of it. *A business thing, strictly!* As for the other, what had caused that, he couldn't be sure now. And even the Jungle Jim outfit wasn't helping there.

Then Anita found a girlfriend called Red who, with her husband, ran a campground on a branch of the Devil River a few miles south of them. "They're so darn enterprising, those two!" she'd say. "They have so much on the ball, real go-getters, I'm telling you!"

But Tommy didn't want to hear. This new kick, this new high, coming after her slump over the past weeks, scared him. Why couldn't she settle down and do some real work to help the place? It seemed there always had to be some big distraction, some big-deal excitement in order for her to be happy, in high gear. Now it was Red and Kevin.

"It's like with food, you know? People need food," she'd say. "They have to pay for food, no matter what. And they also need a place to stay. It's not a *luxury* item, like dinosaurs!"

A place to stay. These words led to worries about the coming northern Michigan winter. The Big Test.

"What do they do winters?"

"That's the beauty of it! They go to Florida and operate a camp-ground down there! But you've got to see their place, Tommy. There's a swimming pool, even. A big, fat, indoor, heated swimming pool—for the campers!"

A swimming pool.

"And a cute launderette neat as a pin. And these great bathrooms with big showers, and everything really clean."

Jesus, he said to himself. Launderette. Bathrooms.

"And canoes, and everything so well kept up. That's the thing. All the grounds, the grass. There's this huge cobblestone fireplace in a big gathering room. Knocks you for a loop when you see it. Better than the Holiday Inn! Honest to God."

"They must have the bucks."

"Sure. Or else investors."

Investors. A word as foreign to him as *stegosaurus* had been. He went into the cool mustiness of his bedroom—it always reminded him of walking back into the 1930s—and thought how the place would be great for people who liked the idea of roughing it for a week or two. But for the real thing—*no*, ten times *no.*

When Anita managed to get them all invited to a cookout at Green Waters, Kevin—and not the cobblestone fireplace—knocked him for a loop. The man, not young, was lean and rugged-looking. His black hair and moustache showed a lot of gray, but it seemed more like silver filings lodged there, glittering. Tommy watched Anita while Red and Kevin gave them a tour and knew Anita was a goner. He was too, nearly. Red was a flame in her yellow sundress, backless except for some flimsy crisscrossing straps. When she talked to him, he imagined solar flares zooming toward him, long fingers of heat. The freckles under her suntan were little embers. When she talked to Anita, she was giggly and confiding. It was quite an act. He was surprised Anita bought it.

They had huge steaks, fancy salads, and bottle after bottle of some imported beer, and then a cold dessert which Anita later told him was chocolate mousse. There'd been too much of everything—food, beer, talk, looking, praising, comparing. Lying in his bed, trying to erase the day, Tommy felt the dead, dragging weight of useless things, impossible hopes, wrong choices. Then Anita was in the room, tipping the bedsprings as she got in beside him.

"I drank too much," she whispered. "My thoughts are racing like crazy."

"Mine, too."

"I'm so depressed I could kill myself."

"Don't say that."

"I know it. You shouldn't let it get to you. But I was thinking, why don't we sell? Get your money out, anyway, and maybe we could try something else."

"A campground?"

"Yeah, right."

They were lying in a little well of mattress, each braced against the other on an incline. At long intervals a car or semi passed, a large sound or small, then crickets and other night creatures took over again. He imagined them living out their insect lives in his woods— and being happy enough.

"The thing is, Tommy, I'm scared. There's not much of a future here, you know? I mean, Christ, what're we gonna do over the winter? We'll go nuts."

He thought of their paths and new bridges, the dinosaurs all painted nice. The snack bar, the woods, the good air. And he knew what an allosaurus was. A brachiosaurus and a stegosaurus. He named all the other names he knew, picturing each of them. "I still think we can make a go of this place," he said finally, but she was asleep, and after a while his dinosaurs pulled him into sleep as well.

In the morning he moved the wrought-iron stairs back up to the belly of his brachiosaurus, which in real life, he'd learned, might have weighed as much as fifty tons. Inside, he sat on a stool he'd brought up without Anita knowing and looked out the side window at cedar branches, and then through the inner window at the *Greatest Heart in the World* picture. No ideas came, but Red and Kevin slipped off into the distance and no longer bothered him. In the daylight, he told himself, things didn't seem so bad.

But then Anita was at the top of the stairs saying, "Listen. I just got this great idea!" Her energy and conviction shot out at him like Red's little signal flares. He could see the three of them packing the car and taking off within the hour.

"What?" he said, not wanting to know.

"Development."

"*What?*"

"Development. A mall. Here! People wouldn't have to drive all the way into town. The summer people, the people in little communities. We'll get some brochures printed and interest some investors, and then—"

"But it's— This is a swamp."

"Fill," she said. "We bring in fill."

"Twenty *acres* of fill?"

"Why are you being so damn negative?" She took a cigarette from a pack she always carried in a leather case, along with her lighter. "What're you doing up here? Going goofy on me?"

"Thinking."

"Well, think about *this*. We gotta wake up and do something, kiddo, or go under. We're not gonna make it on your social security. Simple as that. When something doesn't work, you have to change, adapt, for Chrissake, do something different, or you'll be dead in the water. I could probably get a job in town, but that's nothing. This— This is the *big* time, Tommy. And we've been sitting right on top of it— asleep!"

"You could check it out if you want. See what's what. How much fill costs and so on." He figured the best thing for her would be a project, keeping busy, some kind of plan.

"That's what I like about you." Her tongue flicked out to demolish something on her top lip. "You're a real go-getter."

In the next weeks Anita learned, as she put it, more than she wanted to know about government regulations, environmental impact statements, and above all, about state forest preserves. The Dinosaur Gardens, built in the twenties, had been grandfathered in a state forest tract, where malls and trailer parks, stores, subdivisions, private campgrounds, and all such enterprises were not and never would be allowed. The Dinosaur Gardens could only be what it was—a garden for dinosaurs. "In perpetuity!" she said. "*Un*-believable. Talk about thwarting progress."

"I could have told you that," Kevin said. "We checked all that out before we put down a penny."

"Live and learn!" she joked, her eyes bright with pain and anger.

There were fall color tours in canoes up and down the Devil River, campfires, swims in the heated pool, cookouts. Anita tried to reciprocate, inviting Red and Kevin for sunset walks at the Gardens, but Red made polite, understandable excuses. One of them always had to be close to the office, the way people were always coming and going or needing something. Then Tommy felt bad about closing the Gardens for all those hours and so stayed behind, waiting for tourists, while Anita and Billy spent weekend afternoons and evenings at Green Waters. Who could blame her? he asked himself. But it was like carrying somebody around with him on his shoulders, and he was tired all the time. When a carload of tourists happened to stop, or, once, two older ladies carrying handbooks, he said, "Have fun, there's lots to see," and turned away. He began wearing his old flannel shirts again, and the green work pants.

A large basket of chrysanthemum daisies arrived one afternoon with a card saying, *Congratulations on Your New Venture and Best Wishes for the Future!* "Who the heck's Ernie Dinwiddle?" Anita asked, reading the card, but Tommy didn't know either. "Probably some guy I met at the Chamber of Commerce or something," she said, and put the basket on the snack bar, then forgot to water the flowers. The basket, with its withered stems, red bow, and note stuck to a plastic prong, stayed on the counter, becoming as invisible to them as the napkin dispensers, salt and pepper shakers, and plastic menus.

Then, on a day of heavy wind, low cloud, and snow flurries, Red and Kevin stopped to say good-bye. There were warm promises to keep in touch, to get together again next spring. Their promises, not his. It was Anita's turn, then, to grieve. With Red and Kevin just a few miles away, she at least had a little spark. Now seeing them inches apart in bucket seats, their neat trailer in tow, Anita became teary. "I'll miss you guys!" And they said they'd miss her too, and Billy, but Kevin was already glancing toward the empty highway dusted with snow.

Their leaving coincided with the end of Indian summer and the beginning of wet, cold autumn. Anita was restless yet complained of exhaustion. She began going into town again and coming back later and later—"lit," as Tommy put it to himself. He had a few himself, between jobs, little rewards. And there was more than enough work for him—all of it necessary if they were to make it through.

He bought a caulk gun and tubes of caulking for the windows. Sakrete to repair the crumbling chinks between logs. Roof tar. A long-handled brush for cleaning stovepipe. New chains for his chain saw, with which he added to his log piles. He regarded the squat cast-iron stove with an anxiety bordering on despair, then told himself it might be cozy. But to have to go out in a storm to make a meal in the snack bar? The plumbing and toilets worried him even more. He bought pipe wrap and pipe insulation and heat tape, spending money, he told the clerk in a hardware place, hand over fist. He tried telling himself it was better than sitting in a bar someplace, which is what he'd be doing, otherwise.

A freeze hit. Leaves ripping off, gusting, a whirl of them everywhere. Snow squalls. His woods thinned, letting in gray light. His dinosaurs looked goofy to him, oblivious in their poses. They reminded him of a game he'd played as a kid—"Statues." You whirled around until dizzy, then fell, freezing in some stupid pose that made the other kids laugh. That's how it was, he told himself now. Whirl, whirl, whirl, then some idiotic pose forever. Lonely, with Billy in school and Anita in town, he walked his paths, stopping once in a while to tell Jake or Verna these thoughts. At the mammoth's pond he told the hunters to lay off and give the guy a break. On a milder day in late November, he sat on one of his benches, in thin sunlight, and watched a cloud of insects making their tiny cyclone motions around one another. Night would come and that would be it, he knew, for them. "*Sayonara*, guys," he said, finally, and went back to split more wood.

The contents of the note didn't surprise him, but the note itself did. He hadn't figured she would pick that way, go without telling him.

And she probably told Billy to keep quiet about it, too, which hurt. He found another note on his pillow. *Dear Tommy, I took some of the little dinosaurs from the snack bar. Anita said it would be OK. I'll miss you. Love, Billy.*

The springs swayed under him as he lay back, one leg hanging over the side. Who cared if he could make it up or not. Her car wouldn't be pulling in. Possibilities presented themselves—the main one being the Dry Dock bar in town. But then he remembered he had no car. He got up eventually by rolling onto his side and scrabbling around for a while. He climbed the stairs to the brachiosaurus' belly, shut the door behind him, and sat on his stool. Everything hurt—head, hip, fingertips, eyes, eyebrows, brain. He remembered the insects that morning, and a thought formed: *We are all miniatures.* He could see it on a sign, maybe along one of his paths. People could think what they wanted about it as they walked along. He could make up some others, like the old Burma Shave signs.

The Greatest Heart in the World—

Dead as a doornail.

So what gives?

What's the story?

Hope sparked, then died. He opened the door and kicked the stairway to the side—a rattly, tinny crash. A few yellow poplar leaves were twirling in the breeze. Except for the knocked-over stairway, everything was the same.

He could see a coyote creeping in, cautious. Then some racoons. Crows and turkey buzzards hopping closer. Then moles, mice, and ants cleaning up. Flies. Then snow. Then nothing.

Oh, Jesus.

Headlines: *Man Falls From Dinosaur.*

He sat down in the doorway, letting his legs dangle. If he didn't do it right, he'd wind up an invalid for who knows how long. If he'd jumped right away, it might be all over by now. Too darn much thinking! That was his problem, always.

The weak sun fell behind the brachiosaurus, and cloud cover and wind moved in. Tree limbs clattered. He thought he heard a car door slam and listened hard. Nothing.

He stood and closing his eyes, let go of the doorway. "*Sayonara,* guys," he said, sad to think the swamp would get the dinosaurs again. But the wind seemed to be doing odd things and he grabbed onto the door frame again to listen. *Whoo-oo,* it said. *Whoo-oo!* He opened his eyes. Somebody on the path, coming toward him. Somebody in heavy boots and trousers and puffy jacket. Hope dissolved. This person also wore a squashed-down tan hat and carried a straw bag over one shoulder. Ashamed, he tried to hide.

"Excuse me! Excuse me, sir!"

He had to go to the doorway, surprised to see an older woman in that explorer get-up.

"I didn't think you were here!" she said. "Are you still open for the season?"

"That's a good question." Her thick round eyeglasses reminded him of binoculars. A flush crept up his neck, burning his ears.

"You've gotten yourself in some predicament, sir. I see that now!"

"The wind," he said. "I was up here working. The wind can get real bad."

She looked at the fallen stairs. "It must have been."

Before he could think of another lie, she had the stairs up and was climbing them with great agility. "How unique! In the belly of the brachiosaurus, are you?"

"And pretty darn chewed up, too." His laugh sounded like a crazy man's to him. His ears pulsed with heat. The binocular-glasses were taking in everything—windows, the *Greatest Heart* picture, him. The stems of her glasses were attached to an elastic strap—the kind athletes wear—and he knew why, the way she was tipping her head up, then down, then sideways like some bird trying to see a thing from every angle. A weirdo, in his book. Then she was telling him about the brachiosaurus' leg and pelvic structures, the length of its neck and tail, and how the brachiosaurus probably lived all over North America, possibly in deep pools of water. Behind the glasses, her eyes were wide-set, a gray all lighted up—he got an image of little night-lights burning back in there, and the machinery always working. The eyes fixed on him as she went on and on, telling him of the latest fossil discoveries in Montana and how older, long-respected theories were now being contested left and right. Warm-blooded, not cold-blooded!

Nurturing, gregarious herd creatures, and not solitaries! Swift-moving, not stupidly slow and clumsy! "So you see—just when we think we know something for sure. Have it all worked out. That's what delights me to no end."

"I see what you mean." It figures, he was thinking. Run a freaky place and what do you get?

She descended the stairs, hardly giving them a thought, it seemed, and that amazed him. She had to be his age or more. At least.

"Ernie Dinwiddle," she said, on the ground, and held out her hand. "Short for Ernestine. And you, sir?"

What could he do but tell her, and then tag along while she gave him a guided tour of his own property, talking not only about the dinosaurs, but also about moss, lichens, soil, pinecones, tree bark, stones, moths, and newly-set buds. It was taking forever. The words were one thing and probably would drive a person nuts in no time, he thought, if it weren't for the way she looked at everything. And when she knelt down in leaves that could be hiding anything and began rummaging in the black dirt, his heart started aching worse than his hip. Her splotched and veiny hands looked like brown leaves themselves, cupping the swamp muck, then showing him something probably important though he didn't know what he was supposed to be looking at.

"Oh, this is such a wonderful place! You know, I came here earlier this summer with a dear friend and we'd hoped to talk to you then. We wanted to congratulate you on all the improvements."

"Yeah," he said, "and it's for sale. Maybe you'd be interested in buying it?" Hope churned.

"For sale? But didn't you just purchase it?"

"I bought it to fix up. An investment."

She turned the binoculars on him and he felt spotted with the lie.

Owning such a place was impossible for her, she told him. As for managing a business, well, that was out of the realm, too. She had other priorities and no time, now, for business.

"You lucked out there." He offered her coffee, and in the snack bar thawed some frozen doughnuts.

"The last good days," she said, looking out cloudy windows at the woods, "are always so difficult, aren't they? You simply don't want to go in."

When she again turned to him, he was still trying to think of something to say to that. The way she was staring at him, he felt like one of her stones. All dead weight. He wished he were lying down on his mushy springs and mattress. He wished he could close his eyes. With great effort he said, "What do you do winters, up here? Or do you go south?"

"Oh no! I love my little house, Mr. Vieczorek. I stay up here. Hole up."

"How the heck you manage?"

"Read, for one thing. There's so much to know. No end to it! A person can't know enough."

What for? he wanted to ask. What's the point?

She tapped her forehead. "Soon, this is going to go." She touched her eyeglasses. "And these." She raised her hands. "And these, too. Arthritis, probably. Or Parkinson's. Any number of things. A hundred things can go wrong at any time. The wonder is that they don't—for so long!"

The pins howled. He shifted on the chair to ease his hip. "Well, I might be here, too," he said. "Maybe holing up."

"Maybe?"

She knows! the pins jeered. She sees right through you! "Yeah. Maybe." The ache inside broke outward, making his voice wobble. "I don't know. What's next, I mean." Glancing around to escape the binoculars, he saw the basket of dead flowers, the bow, the note, the name there. Oh, Jesus, he said to himself.

"It hasn't been a good season, then?"

"Not exactly." He laughed to hide the wobble, the weakening. "It was a mistake, if you want to know. This place. People today, they want Star Wars stuff, Disneyland, but that's not it, that's not what—" The pitch of his voice scared him now, the tightening everywhere— throat, heart, blood vessels, it seemed, shrinking to nothing. "The thing is— It's just that a person gets to the point where you, ah, see the end, you know? The end of the line." He took hold of his coffee mug to anchor his hand. All his life he'd lived by the rule that it never paid to show weakness, but what did it matter when you're going to get stomped anyway? "For me," he said, "this is the end."

"The end?"

"Yeah. I gotta face it. That's all."

"So."

"As I see it, the only choice I have at this point is—" Oh, shut up, he told himself. Stop whining! "You want more coffee?"

"Please. It's my one vice. But I'm hoping you will be here. I wanted to ask if I might come and walk a few times a week. I've done that for several winters now. These trails are just right for the exercise one needs."

"Walk?"

"On snowshoes. That way, you see, I can walk all winter."

"Ah." He didn't have snowshoes, he told her, trying to be polite, but it sounded like a pretty good idea.

"It is! It's wonderful. You must try it."

That'll be the day, he wanted to say, but humoring her—she meant well, after all—he went into a long story about his hip, the operations, the pins, the trouble, now.

"But it's just walking—on snow. It would be just the thing for you. And I have," she said, "an extra pair of snowshoes."

He saw himself in his safari outfit, his feet strapped to things that resembled tennis rackets. Un-believable! he heard Anita saying.

"Ah—that's OK. Thanks anyway. You go right ahead, though."

"Splendid! And perhaps you'll reconsider."

Splendid. Never had he heard that word spoken—not even on TV. Never could he have imagined it might apply to anything having to do with him. *Splen-*did.

"I could fix us something nice," she said. "For a winter picnic. You know! A wineskin. Some good cheese, nice crisp bread, cold cuts. I sometimes do that just for myself. Then if anything happened, I could last for a while, anyway. I always carry matches, too. And a good-sized piece of heavy plastic."

"Plastic?"

"It's a marvelous windbreak and keeps you quite warm."

"So you'd have a picnic, then, worse comes to worst."

"Oh no! For a picnic you need one other person, at least."

He looked at his new guide, the flush coming again, and tried to imagine it—a picnic in the snow. Wine, bread, cheese, lunch meat, his doughnuts.

"Well," he heard himself saying, "I could maybe bring some beer." Oh, stupid, stupid! the pins railed at him. Think of the nonstop talk. Think what you're getting into *now*, you jerk. She's lonely and just pulled a fast one, is what! But he said, "And maybe some doughnuts." Shifting, he placed one hand on his sore hip, trying to stop the racket there. "Wonderful," he heard her saying, "but we don't have to wait for winter, you know. Especially if this good weather holds!"

"Oh, by the way," he said at her car, "I want to thank you for those flowers. That was real nice."

"Well, Mr. Viecorek, this is real nice, too. So we're even."

"Tommy," he said. "Call me Tommy, if you want. Everybody does."

"Splendid!"

At sunset it was still too mild to go in, and he walked his trails, thinking how he wouldn't have to wear the Jungle Jim suit now and she wouldn't mind—in her squashed hat and baggy trousers and boots. Oh, unbelievable, the things he got himself into! But for the first time in weeks he saw how nice the paths really did look, winding through the swamp and making it all a kind of weird garden of ferns and rocks and streams and a million other things that were somehow all his. *Un*-believable, Tommy. *Splen*-did!

Passing his dinosaurs, he told them they didn't have to worry, not for a while anyway. He, Tommy V., was still around and kicking. On the way back, he sat on the bench near Tony, his triceratops, its three horns angled fiercely toward the darkening woods. Watching shadows grow, he imagined he could see her there, at the edge of the clearing, digging around in the mud and leaves. A few flying insects found him and did their cyclone dance, and from the mammoth's pond came the pulsing of crickets. But he heard something else, too. What? He stiffened, concentrating on the new sound. Someone coming? *Something* coming? A bear? A wolf, maybe? Or a rattler crawling through leaves and wood chips? He looked at Tony, who seemed to know something was up as well. He looked at the wood chips. Nothing—that he could see. He looked toward the woods, where it was too dark to see anything at all. *Soon these are going to go, Ernie told him again, touching her thick glasses, and not being afraid—or so it'd seemed. Well, he wasn't either, he told Tony, and went to the edge of the clearing to listen.*

A crackling and crumbling, but so faint under the sounds of breeze and crickets and his own breathing and the bumping of his heart. Something like the smallest doors in the world creaking open one after another. Then he was kneeling, his bad hip shooting pain everywhere, swamp water seeping through his work pants, and a boggy smell wafting up. It was crazy as anything, he knew, but the sound seemed to be coming from the leaves, the ground, and could only be what she'd shown him—all those tiny things digging in, now, with little root feet no bigger than hairs and hanging on for all they were worth.

THE COURTSHIP
OF WIDOW SOBCEK

Warmed by his feather-tick, John Jielewicz lay in bed and studied the ceiling. What day was it? Then he knew, and time began once more. Saturday. Overcast and dull. It looked like snow. He got up quickly, made coffee, and set to work. After washing his cup and saucer, he mopped the linoleum in the kitchen and bathroom, dusted the spools of his furniture, and vacuumed the rose-patterned rugs of his living room. Then he rinsed out his opalescent glass spittoon in the base-ment. His housecleaning finished for the week, he filled the bathtub, threw in his long underwear and shirt, and lowered himself into the hot water. The day was half gone.

Steam clouded the mirror, and late afternoon light illumined pale swans and lily pads floating on turquoise wallpaper. He considered the week. On Monday he'd spaded the garden, and on Tuesday he'd chopped wood. He'd worked at Chet's on Wednesday and Thursday, making polish sausage and pickled bologna. Then on Friday— But what had he done on Friday? The stoker? No. The garage? No. The car? The yard? No. What then? How could he forget in just one day? The stoker? No. The basement, the stoker, the coal? Yes, the coal!

He'd taken the Plymouth to Townsend's and ordered a ton of coal. Then he'd come home, checked the coal bin, and swept the basement.

It was good to think of the work ahead. Soon Chet would be getting big Christmas orders for smoked hams and sausages, and he would be busy. Years of working with casings in icy water and handling cold meats had twisted his hands, and they ached with changes in the weather. He held them beneath the hot water. Next to his thin legs, as white and veined as church marble, his hands looked like gnarled stumps. But they were good hands, he thought, hardworking hands. And he'd done his share of work in his time—the lumber camps, the farm, the store. What else was there besides work? People sometimes said, "That John Jielewicz. He sure knows how to work!" That made him pull back his narrow shoulders and walk proudly.

"Pa," his daughter had said on one of her Sunday night visits, "move in with us." Casting her eyes around the big rooms, she'd said, "Why all this work, Pa? You don't need so much work at your age. And for what? Who sees it?"

Removing his pipe, he'd said, "I see it." Then he'd leaned over his chair to spit into the spittoon, defying all the ranch houses on the south side of town.

The bath water was getting tepid and uncomfortable; he added more hot water, soaped himself with a bar of Fels Naptha, and ducked his head twice under the water. Then he soaped the underwear and the shirt, rinsed them, and pulled the plug.

Later, dressed in clean clothes, his hair parted in the center and combed down flat like feathers, he cleaned the tub and hung his washing on a line running between plum trees in back. Then it was time for confession.

Driving to church in his Plymouth, he took stock. Anger? Yes. Cursing? Yes. Lying? No, never. Any of the others? No. For years he'd confessed his sins to Monsignor Gapzinski, and the old priest knew him by name. "John," he'd said once, before giving the absolution, "You're a strong, good man, but think about Our Lord's words, 'He who exalts himself shall be humbled.'" Later, in a dim pew, he'd made his penance of one rosary but hadn't bothered about the words. When he'd finished the last decade of the rosary and blessed himself, he rose and walked proudly past lines of people still waiting to confess.

That night, the lines seemed much slower. After a long wait, he finally entered the confessional, and when the panel slid open before his eyes, he began in Polish. But an unfamiliar voice interrupted, asking if he could speak English.

Startled, he asked, "Where is Monsignor?"

"He's ill," the unfamiliar voice whispered. "Please pray for him. I'm Father Jim, and I'll be filling in for a while."

How could it be, he wondered. Monsignor sick? Such a good man, too. The unfamiliar voice again interrupted, asking him to begin his confession in English, if he could.

"I was angry this week," he said. "I cursed." He stopped and waited for the priest's response. His eyes adjusting to the darkness, he could just make out a black crucifix and a hearing-aid device on the wall before him.

After some time, the priest said, "And is that all?"

When he didn't speak, the priest went into a lengthy sermon. His voice rising above a whisper, he talked of flames of love and flames of anger; he talked of charity and of God's love. The words ran together, and unable to keep up with their flow, John lost interest and thought instead of what he would do after Mass the next day. The Lord's Day was not for work, he knew, but a little raking couldn't be called work. He'd raked his own leaves several times, but leaves from neighbors' yards were always blowing into his. He would do a little raking; then maybe he would put another coat of varnish on the woodwork in the archway. He liked wood to be shiny.

The priest broke into his reverie. "Do you understand the nature of your penance, then?"

"Excuse me?" he said in Polish.

"English, please," the priest said loudly.

"I'm sorry. I don't hear you."

The priest raised his voice even more. "Instead of regular penance, which implies punishment," he said, "I would like you to try thinking—all this coming week—of God's love for you. Whenever you can, think of His goodness and of the goodness of life. Do this when you feel anger or when you wish to curse. Do you understand?"

Astonished and confused, he couldn't speak.

"Good," said the priest after a moment. He gave the absolution, the Latin rushing like water.

Then the small wooden panel slid shut, and he was finished. Outside the confessional, he thought people stared at him; he lowered his eyes. Lights burned only near the confessional, and farther up the nave he could kneel in half-light. He took his usual pew and out of habit began his rosary. But blessing himself with the metallic cross, he suddenly remembered that it wasn't his penance. What was it, then? Something about love when he felt like cursing. No, that wasn't it. It was something about God and love, flames and cursing. He couldn't get it right. Now how do you like that, he said to himself, feeling anger grow. To make matters worse, his stomach started acting up, burning and heaving. He turned around to survey the waiting lines. People were standing as if frozen in the aisles. He looked to the front of the church; the statues, in shadow, seemed miles away. The sanctuary lamp burned red. He was angry now and unsettled; he didn't feel like a new man. It was the priest's fault. The priest had ruined it, and he wouldn't be able to receive Communion tomorrow. I'm not about to stand in line all over again, he told himself. I may as well work tomorrow, then, and be damned.

After a supper of lard on bread, cold sausage, and coffee diluted with milk, he rocked in his dimly lit living room. Smoking his pipe and spitting into the clean spittoon, he mulled over the priest's words—the few he remembered. They seemed like clues or pieces of a puzzle, and he wished he'd listened better. Flames, he said to himself. Flames and love, whatever that meant. Well, he knew about flames, that's for sure. As if it had happened the day before, he saw his white-eyed team of horses rearing up against a sky black as hell with smoke. Half-mad himself, he'd fought the crazed beasts to a standstill while Masha got things into the wagon. He knew about flames. But flames and love and how it tied together with cursing, he couldn't figure out.

Cursing. Now there was his failing. He'd never forgotten the time a storm caught him plowing. The steel-blue sky cracked apart in a dozen places, and the horses lunged, toppling the plow. Straddling a furrow of stony earth, he'd cursed the lightning and the horses, the plow and the field. He'd called on a hundred demons. It seemed he could touch one of the bolts, so close they came, snaking into the earth. The air stank with sulphur. He got the plow unhitched and ran

with the horses while rain made rivers of the furrows. In the house
Masha, pale as death, was running from room to room, dipping her
fingers in a jar of holy water and sprinkling the walls, the floors, the
babies. Still cursing, he stood dripping wet in the kitchen, while rain
blew in the open windows and glasses rattled in the cupboards. Masha
ran into the kitchen and sprinkled water on him. Just then, a stream
of light poured in one window and out the other, burning the very
air. It had snaked across the entire kitchen, missing them by inches.
Masha, her hand held out as if paralyzed, water still dripping from her
fingers, had only said, "See John? See what your cursing brings?" For a
long time after that, he hadn't dared to curse.

How could anything like that be connected with love? he wondered. The new priest must be a little touched. Masha had been a
little touched, too. She'd been a good woman, a good worker, but
too holy. Once, she came back from the village and went straight
into the parlor without saying a word. There, she lit a candle before
the statue of the Virgin and then sat, still as a stone, before that little
flame. He'd called her and had even asked if she was sick. But there
she sat, pale as death. She wouldn't answer him; she wouldn't even
look at him. She held a rosary in her lap, but her fingers didn't move
over the beads. The parlor grew darker and colder as the day lost its
light, and the candle burned more brightly in that dimness. It cast
shadows over the Virgin's mantle, and it seemed the figure was moving. Frightened, he left her alone in the room. Finally, long after the
candle had guttered out, Masha appeared in the kitchen. He was making pancakes, and flour dusted the planks under the table.

"John," she'd said, scared as a child. "I seen her."

"Who?"

"The Virgin."

"No."

"Oh yes. On the timber cut going to the church."

He was quiet, afraid of what more she might say.

"She was so bright, I fell down and covered my face. I cried because
she was so beautiful, so beautiful."

He hadn't liked it one bit. People would say she was touched, and it
wouldn't look good. But he'd been surprised when just the opposite
happened. People started saying she was a saint. That made him

proud of her, even though he didn't think she was a saint. She was just a woman. Couldn't they see that?

As he smoked and waited for bedtime, he looked around the room. His oval wedding picture, his plant in the alcove, his clock, all were sunk in shadow. Shadows blurred the shape of his wife's rocker at the end of the double living room. Sometimes, depending on the play of shadows, it seemed the rocker moved, as if brushed by a wind. "Sleep, Masha, sleep," he would say then. When the clock on the closed gramophone struck ten times, he rapped his pipe against the spittoon and abandoned the living room to darkness. His back resting on a pad of sheepskin, his thin body covered by a heavy feather-tick, he too slept. Outside, the underwear stiffened and moved on the line like a ghost in a frost-blasted garden.

That night he slept badly, and all the next day unfinished business plagued him. At Mass he'd sat in the pew—like a bump on a log, he thought—while everybody else went to Communion. By the time his daughter came for her visit, his stomach was good and sour.

"So, Pa," she said. "What did you do today?" She wore a Sunday dress too tight about the waist.

"Do?" he said irritably. One leg made a sharp angle over the hassock. "There's always something to do around here." The smell of fresh varnish still hung in the air.

"Pa, come live with us. We'd like you to." She motioned at the lofty ceilings, the corners. "There's just too much work here."

She's lying, he thought. How could they want him? His stomach turned, and a sour liquid rose in his throat.

"Son of a bitch!" he said in Polish. "I need my powders."

He left her alone in the living room.

When he returned from the bathroom, she said, "Pa, go see a doctor with that stomach of yours. 'Powders'! What are these 'powders' you get at Wiesneski's? Go see a real doctor."

In one sharp Polish sentence, he cast all doctors into the flames of hell. Then he took up his pipe and calmly rocked while his daughter struggled into her coat.

"At least," she said, standing, "why not sell and get something smaller, maybe closer to us?"

"Bah," he said, and spat into the spittoon.

Then she was gone, and he heard her old Hudson start up in the driveway. In the quiet he smoked and rocked and studied his plant. Masha was the one who could grow plants, he thought. She could make sticks grow, while he had to fight the damned soil for each and every potato. He'd been waiting a long time now for those bright blue and orange flowers promised in the catalogue. It'll be a cold day in hell, he thought. Behind the plant, the radiators hissed. It's too damned dry in here, he decided, and went to the kitchen for water.

After watering the plant and filling the cake pans set on the radiators for humidity, he had time for another smoke. Letting his thoughts go where they would, he remembered old Mr. Smigelski. Once Mrs. Raniszewski had said after church, "Merry Christmas, Mr. Smigelski!" Bowing, the crazy fool shouted, "Ass to me, ass to you!" How she'd looked when he said that! Every time he saw Smigelski after church, he was tempted to say, "Ass to me, ass to you, you crazy fool!" He said the words as they were intended: *As to me, as to you*. Now what did that mean? Whatever happens to me, let it happen to you? Or, what you say to me, let me say to you? That must be it. The crazy fool! He laughed just thinking about it.

When the clock chimed ten times, he rapped his pipe on the spittoon and rose from the rocker. Before turning off the floor lamp, he saw that his lace curtains were getting yellow. It was time to take them to the Widow Sobcek.

But he forgot about the curtains during the week; there was too much other work to think about. The stoker clogged somehow, and he had to crawl around in the dust, fixing it. Then four shingles blew off the roof, and he dragged out his wooden ladder from the garage. Extended its full thirty-five feet, it was just long enough to reach the north gable. Up he went, hand over hand, with shingles, hammer, and nails in a cloth bag at his side. The ladder was springy; wind puffed his jacket and blew in his face. If it should slip, he thought, imagining the old ladder sliding sideways across the clapboard, sending him and his damned shingles all to hell. But it didn't slip, and he finished the job.

Only when he was back down on the frozen ground did he feel his legs trembling. Dragging the ladder back into the garage, he was proud of himself. It'd been a job worth doing.

On Saturday, he remembered the curtains. After his housecleaning and his bath, he pulled a straight-back chair to the radiators. Standing on the chair, he freed the curtain rods, pulled off the stiff panels, and let them fall into a wicker basket. "Damn it to hell," he said at the dust. "Pfoo!" He got down and surveyed the bare windows. They looked empty, like Mrs. Kranak's windows during Lent. She took down her curtains on Ash Wednesday and didn't put them back up until Holy Saturday. Her empty dark windows reminded him of something; he wasn't sure just what, but it wasn't good. How could she stand it all those weeks? On Easter Sunday he was relieved to see her white curtains against the wavering panes of glass. Looking at his own windows, he saw he would have to wash them on Monday. The stained-glass pieces at the top were dusty and dull; the window panes were streaked and murky. Before leaving for the widow's he had to wash dust from his hands.

Turning his green Plymouth off First Avenue, he drove into a neighborhood of plain houses, fenced gardens, and small yards. No stained glass in the windows; no fancy fretwork on the gables. All was simple and neat and stark in the late afternoon light. The bare yards had a wintry look, and children in winter jackets and caps played in old piles of leaves.

He drove slowly over broken concrete, conscious of his sour stomach. It was churning and heaving. That morning he'd put a spoonful of butter into his coffee and took an extra measure of the powders, but nothing did the trick. He had a sudden thought, as jarring as a glimpse of a snake disappearing in a rock pile. *What if this is some great sickness?* The thought shook him, but gripping the steering wheel, he told himself: *No, by God. Not yet. Not John Jielewicz!*

Scowling, he parked his Plymouth on gravel in front of the widow's house. The streets had no curbs in her neighborhood. His scowl deepened when he recognized, parked just ahead, the shiny beast of a car that always reminded him of a hearse. It belonged to Mrs. Stanley, a divorced woman with black hair and red fingernails. "*Czarownica!*" he said, lifting his basket from the back seat. She was a proud, mean witch, and it bothered him to think the widow washed the woman's curtains. He would never do that.

There was room for only one at a time on the narrow sidewalk, and he had to wait for Mrs. Stanley to pass. She carried white curtains over one arm, a white veil over the black fur of her coat. As she passed, hairs on the coat rose, like a dog's, and caught the light. He scowled, but she ignored him. His stomach heaved and fluttered.

Waiting on the porch, he looked over the widow's yard. Bare maple limbs interlocked above raked grass, and mounds of leaves were heaped over the garden. Low gray clouds in the west reflected pale colors. Earlier every day now, he said to himself, thinking of the sunset.

A small woman wearing a bib apron over a flower-print dress opened the door. "Mr. Jielewicz," she said, "good to see you." She held the door for him, then closed it. Inside, she wiped steam from her glasses. "How are you?"

He set his basket near a drying frame holding a stretched curtain and thought of the black coat and of his stomach. "I'm no good," he said. "No damned good." He looked around the small kitchen. As always, the widow's linoleum was polished, and the windows were steamed up from washing and cooking. In one window she had hung three glass shelves for African violets, and he could see, behind the purple flowers, a gloomy December sky. "I will sit a while and rest," he told her.

"That's good," she said. "Sit. I will rest, too." But holding the back of a kitchen chair for support, she made her way to the stove. There, a bowl and plate had been warming, and she poured *kvass* and cut two pieces of bread from a loaf cooling on the cupboard.

Slowly, she moved between stove and table, carrying the bowl before her like an offering. She made a second trip for the plate of bread and a spoon. "Eat, Mr. Jielewicz," she said. "Eat and feel better."

He stirred the rich brown soup, with its raisins and prunes and *kluski* like small clouds. When did he last have *kvass* like that, he wondered. Steam rose from the bowl. Masha, he thought. Masha had made *kvass* like that. Ten years in March, then. Taking a blue handkerchief from his pocket, he wiped his brow and very quickly his eyes. When he finished the soup, he looked up. The widow was watching him.

"It's good," he said. "It settled my stomach."

"Have more," she said. Both hands on the arms of her chair, she slowly lifted herself up. Her legs were wrapped in layers of support stockings, as thick as children's winter leggings.

"Sit," he said, getting up. "I can wait on myself."

While he finished the second bowl of *kvass*, the widow began attaching a curtain to a drying frame, carefully inserting small pins through the lace to preserve its design.

"Do you get tired doing that every day?" he asked.

"Oh," she said, "yes and no. Some days, when my legs hurt, yes. Today, no." Then she gathered a curtain from the basket and, holding up one end, let it fall between them. "Each so different, so beautiful," she said, "that I don't get so tired."

Through the white lace he saw a young girl. Like— But he blocked the thought. Startled, he felt blood rush to his face. Then she let the curtain fall into the basket, and the Widow Sobcek appeared again, gray hair and glasses, the housedress and thick stockings.

Behind the African violets, the sky was growing darker. It was time to leave. He sighed as he put four dollar bills on the oilcloth. She took two of the bills, tucked them into her apron pocket, then pushed the remaining bills toward him. "Take," she said, as she always did when he overpaid. "Take. I don't need."

Driving from the widow's in the December dusk, he saw that it would snow. All was still and cold and gray. In time for evening confession, he drove down side streets and took stock. Anger? Yes. When? He remembered—that fool of a priest, the penance left undone. Now what? The Plymouth slowed and came to a stop in the middle of a block. He would get worked up, he thought, going back to that priest. He waited for his stomach to start acting up, but it was strangely quiet. Should he go home or should he try it again? On the windshield flakes of snow appeared, hanging there like the widow's white lace. *So beautiful*, she'd said. He thought of the priest's words—the clues he'd tried to figure out. The Plymouth began to roll forward. He turned on the windshield wipers, and the stone-gray road appeared under the headlights. At the intersection of First and Maple, he turned right, toward the church.

It was nearly a year later when his daughter said, on a Sunday evening, "Oh, Pa, everyone's talking about you. It's awful."

He heard sleet at the windowpanes, a low whispering sound. He leaned over his chair and spat into the spittoon. He drew on his pipe before speaking. Then he said, "*Plotka!*"

"No," she said. "Not gossip. They're right to talk. It's crazy, that's what it is. Here you are running over there every week with curtains! Everyone's laughing, but I don't think it's so funny. I think it's—"

"Not every week."

"No, but you know what I mean. Every month, then. Just as bad. Don't look at me like that. I'm not the one to blame. People are saying a lot of things. They're saying that . . . that you don't know what you're doing. Oh, Pa!"

He thought over the words. Well, maybe it was crazy. What would she think if he told her about the lace? Ever since the widow held the lace curtain in the air between them, he'd been seeing lace everywhere. When he cleaned out the stoker, the clinkers looked like lace. So did the ice when he chopped it off the sidewalks. Everywhere lace! At first it bothered him and he worried, but then he got used to the idea and began to look at things to see how close they came to the widow's lace. He was surprised. Sugar in the sugar bowl, the stars at night, even the thorny hedge at his property line. One day while cutting the grass, he saw light coming through little openings in the hedge, and right away he thought *lace!* Shadows of tree limbs on grass, car tracks on snow, birds flying through the air—all reminded him of lace. So did the feathery tops of new carrots and even the rougher edges of cabbage and potato plants. It *was* crazy! One day he made a list of all the things that reminded him of the lace curtain, and he was astounded to find over fifty items. He put the list away in his safe, but added to it every week. Crazy? Well, what of it? He wanted to laugh. Lace everywhere! He would make a joke, and his daughter would laugh, too. "Ass to me, ass to you," he said, thinking of Mr. Smigelski. He laughed, showing brown stubs of teeth.

But she was alarmed, and her eyes flew from him to the oval wedding picture to the alcove. "Oh, Pa," she said, "cut out this silliness! Act your age."

The problem was, he thought, he didn't feel his age; he wanted to be foolish. "If I acted my age," he said, "I'd be dead!" He laughed. At the rate he was going, he would probably find lace in the grave as well!

"Pa," she said thoughtfully, "what did you do with your plant?" She was looking at the empty space in the alcove where his plant on its pedestal had been for years.

The alcove looked larger, he thought, without the plant, and the curtains showed better. Should he tell her? It was last Holy Thursday, he remembered, when he'd taken the plant to the widow's. How she'd laughed when she opened the door. "There's a plant growing out of your head, Mr. Jielewicz," she'd said. He must have looked foolish, with those big gray-green leaves, like rabbit ears, hiding his face.

"Now what are you smiling about," his daughter was saying. "You won't tell me where you took the plant, but I know! I thought I saw it at the widow's when I took my curtains there, and I was right. Only I didn't know it could have such nice flowers. Think what you're doing, Pa. Think of Mama, for heaven's sake." She blew her nose in a Kleenex. "Oh, dear," she said, putting the wad of tissue in her purse. "I have to get home. John has a cold, and I'm getting it. One thing after another. If you moved in with us, like we wanted you to, none of this would be happening." She got her arms into heavy coat sleeves.

How old was she now? he wondered, studying his daughter. She didn't look like the little girl who'd tangled rolls of string at the store and drew pictures on pink butcher paper. He looked to the wedding picture on the shadowy wall. They'd stood so still, so straight, facing the big camera—Masha, young, thin, unsmiling; himself solemn as a minister and thin as a rail in his new suit.

Standing and buttoning her coat, she said, "For heaven's sake, Pa, at your age you don't want to be marrying again."

So, he thought. *So.* He saw the widow in her housedress and felt slippers. A poor woman. He thought of his old safe in his bedroom closet, hidden behind his black suits. His name was printed in gold letters over the combination, but the light in the closet was too dim for it to show. When he opened his safe to get money or to add to his list, he had to use a flashlight. Then he thought: *John.* Who is John? That is my name. He remembered. John was his grandson, a boy he seldom saw, a little boy—small and pale and weak. He wondered why his daughter always left the boy at home when she visited. Not seeing the husband didn't bother him, but he would like to see the boy now and then. He looked at Masha's rocker, but it was still. I should marry again, he thought, and leave them nothing.

His stomach began a faint stir. The gossips. He drew in on the pipe and exhaled a great cloud of smoke. That's what they're worried about. She's speaking for the others. He thought of his two sons and daughter who lived in other states and only visited at Christmas. Then they talked about the bad roads and how the town was going to the dogs. He should marry! The idea was pleasing; how they would worry then! But something intervened. He saw the widow's rough hand pushing the dollar bills toward him. *Take,* she'd said. *Take. I don't need.*

His daughter tied a wool kerchief under her chin and slipped on gloves. "Well, I'm going, Pa," she said. "Don't forget about dinner at our house next week. You said you would come."

She's tired, he thought. He saw her small house on its barren lot, all clutter and light. No comfortable shadows or large rooms. He didn't like going there. But there was something he wanted to do. What was it? The oilcloth. Yes, what else? The dollar bills. Yes. "Wait," he told his daughter. "Wait just a minute."

He left her in the living room as the clock was striking nine-thirty, and returned several minutes later. Dangling car keys from a gloved hand, she stood near Masha's rocker. "You know, Pa, we still have to talk over this other thing."

"Never mind that," he said. "Give this to the boy. Give this to John."

Startled, she took the unsealed envelope and with gloved hands opened it. "Pa!" she said, as she lifted out a thick packet of bills. "What is this craziness? What's the matter with you!" She tried to push the envelope and bills into his hands, but he stepped back.

"Take," he said. "It's for the boy. For school. For anything."

"Oh, Pa!"

In a moment he was encircling her heavy bulk with his bony arms. "Never mind," he said. "Never mind."

Only when she moved back, wiping her eyes, did he notice the bunch of lace at her neck. Gathered with a black velvet ribbon, it fanned out like the top of a carrot.

Holding a bag of salt in one hand, he let go of the ice-coated porch rail, and his feet took to the sky. That's how he explained it to his daughter at the hospital.

"I saw every kind of star," he told her.

"Never mind stars," she said. "You could have broken your back. Then what?"

But he was too tired to answer. His eyelids shut of their own accord, and he saw stars whirling about his head. He dozed. When he opened his eyes, she was still there.

"I'm going home," he said.

"You can't! What do you want to do, Pa? Fall again?"

He wanted to tell her they had no right keeping him in the hospital when he wanted to go home, but the words wouldn't come. Instead, he dozed and saw a big black hearse slowly backing up to an open door. He was on a cart, rolling toward the car's dark cave. Terrified, he opened his eyes.

"I'm going home," he said, struggling to rise. "I have . . . things to do."

She was beside the bed, holding him back. "Pa! You're not supposed to move. Your ribs are all cracked. Look, here's your lunch. And the nurse!"

"Well, Mr. Jielewicz," the nurse said. "Full of pep, are you? The doctor was right. They don't make 'em like you any more."

"I hope not," his daughter said to herself, but he heard.

It seemed his hair was standing up like a shock of hay, so he brushed at it with a stiff, bandaged hand. Shame, shame, he thought, to be lying here like a baby while strangers walked around the bed, looking at him. A young girl wearing a dress of pink stripes swung a narrow table over the bed and set a tray of food on it. He looked at the colors—green, yellow, brown, something red on the side. It looked like his workbench in the basement, where he cleaned his paintbrushes.

"I'm not eating," he said. "I'm going home." He closed his eyes.

"Pa!"

"Don't worry, Mrs. Kirchner," he heard the nurse say. "If he won't eat now, he'll be good and hungry later."

His eyes still closed, he saw himself getting up, putting on his underwear, pants, and shirt, starting the Plymouth and driving home. Then he would— But what day was it? Was it still Wednesday?

"What day is it?" he asked his daughter, as if from a great distance.

"What did you say, Pa? I can't hear you."

"Day," he said. "What day?"

"Day? Oh! Day. It's Saturday."

Saturday! He struggled to put the week back together. On Monday he had— But he couldn't remember that far back. Tuesday, then. On Tuesday he— He worked at Chet's. That's right. It was raining when he drove home. Then it got cold. The next day everything was ice. The trees, the bushes, and the utility wires. The steps and the side of the house. Sunlight was everywhere. Icy tree limbs shone like glass against the blue sky. So bright. So, so bright. He dozed again.

When he awoke, the widow was there, placing a bowl of *kvass* on the table where the tray of food had been.

"I see in the paper about your fall, so I come," she said. "Eat, Mr. Jielewicz. Eat and feel better."

Was he dreaming? But no, steam rose like incense from the bowl, and he could smell the rich soup. His eyes burned. Suddenly he remembered what he'd seen just before the dark. Sunlight on polished steps. And near the edge, where icicles dripped from the roof, designs as fine as flowers. *Lace!* Then his legs flew from under him, and pellets of salt rose in the air like confetti.

One week later, he awoke from a nap and knew it was long after lunchtime. A tray of cold food sat on the bed table. The widow hadn't come; something was wrong. All that week she'd come, bringing him good food—*kvass* and ham, chicken and dumplings, pierogi and apple pie. He watched the doorway and imagined her walking in, wearing the babushka and long, gray coat, the galoshes. The doorway remained empty.

That Monday the doctor had checked him and said he could go home if he promised to be careful. He'd thought a bit and asked the doctor if he could perhaps stay a day or two longer. "Why?" the doctor wanted to know. Then he'd lied. "A little pain yet," he'd said, avoiding the doctor's eyes.

"What time is it?" he asked the girl in pink stripes who brought him a glass of juice.

She looked at her wristwatch. "Three-thirty," she said. "Why? Expecting company?" She laughed, straightened the blankets, then took away the untouched food.

He waited, every minute expecting the widow to appear in her babushka, coat, and galoshes. The curtain soon made a long shadow on his bed, and then he knew she wouldn't come. It was too late. He was wide awake now; something nagged him. What was it? The widow shuffling into the room. Yes. What else? Her long, gray coat and the heavy boots. Yes. And? Then he knew. Dear God, he said to himself, let me burn forever in hell if I have done a bad thing!

He swung his legs out from under the sheet and blanket; when his bare feet touched the cold tile, he was chilled. He stood, feeling sore all over, but he walked to the closet and found his clothing. He recognized the shirt; he'd been wearing it when he fell. It was so long ago, he thought. He undid the white hospital gown and let it fall to the floor. Then he pulled his underwear up over the bandages. He dressed quickly. Hurry, hurry, hurry, he said to himself, tangling his shoelaces. He looked at the other bed, prepared to lie, but his roommate slept, tubes feeding his arms.

At the doorway he cautiously waited for the corridor to clear. He saw nurses talking together at the desk near the elevator. Pretending he was just a visitor, he walked to the elevator and turned his back to them. Doors mysteriously opened, and he stepped into the bright cubicle. Free, he thought, pressing buttons.

In the mild air outside, a taxi waited, as if for him. A taxi! He'd never hired a taxi. Did he have any money? Dear God! He rifled his pockets and found two dollar bills in his pants. Waving the bills in the air, he pounded on the window, startling the driver. He shouted the widow's address.

The driver got out and walked around the car to open the back door. "Well, hop in, then!"

Holding his side, he climbed into the back seat. Hurry, hurry, hurry, he said to himself.

"Nice day," the driver said, starting up a loud clock on the dashboard. "Looks like spring will get here yet."

They were off. He looked out the window and saw puddles of water in the gutters and black-crusted snowbanks in yards. Already the grass seemed green where snow had melted. Hurry, hurry, hurry, he said to himself.

When the driver came to open the door for him, the clock on the dashboard had stopped ticking. "That'll be one dollar and fifty cents," he said.

"Take," he said, thrusting the bills at the man. He rushed up the narrow walk.

At the widow's door he knocked, but there was no answer. He tried the door, and it opened. Stepping inside, he heard her voice coming from the living room. She was lying like a fallen bird, her legs covered with a thick, woolen blanket. What had he done! Dear God in Heaven, strike me dead. Bury me in ashes!

"Mr. Jielewicz!" she said. "What are you doing here?"

His side ached, and he couldn't find breath to speak. Finally, he was able to say, "What is the matter, little lady?"

"Oh," she said, "my legs got tired. Not so bad, but everyone wants clean curtains for Easter, and I can't walk so good now." She sat up and turned on a table light. "Mrs. Stanley come today and says she needs her curtains no later than tomorrow. Now, no curtains."

That witch, he thought, seeing the woman in her black coat. What does she need with clean curtains! Under his bandages everything hurt and burned.

"Tomorrow, I will be better," the widow said, as if she believed it.

He looked at the thick stockings and the felt slippers and knew what he had done. Dear God in Heaven! Too much work, and maybe even walking to the hospital. To see him.

"Where are those curtains?"

"Oh no, Mr. Jielewicz. You can't do them!"

"Tell me how."

In a room off the kitchen he knelt, ignoring a great pain in his side, and plunged his bandaged hands into a washtub of warm water. Steam rose when he lifted a curtain into the air. Water poured off the material, and light from the setting sun made rainbows all over the soapy lace. Dear God! he cried, seeing once again the widow's face behind the veil. In his joy, he nearly upset the tub.

THE IMPORTANCE OF
HIGH PLACES IN A FLAT TOWN

A man belonged with his wife and child and not with an aunt, no matter how old or sick, no matter if she'd brought him up, no matter, even, if the wife was the one who'd taken off first. It was unnatural, hanging around at home like that. It wasn't right. That's what people were saying, Frankie knew. So why not just go? Drive down there and try to work something out. Do whatever. His hands and legs went jittery, as with a caffeine fit, but when Angie came around with the coffee pot, he said, "Sure," and pushed his cup toward her. There's more to it, he was thinking. More to it somehow. Only he didn't know what.

"Frankie," Angie said, "you tell your Aunt Rosa I'm going to get over there to see her one of these days. I been too darn busy, you tell her. How about some more potato pancakes?"

"No," he said. "Thanks. I was just thinking of driving down to Detroit. Crazy, hey?"

She took his plate. "I don't know what to tell you, Frankie. As far as I'm concerned, you're between the devil and the deep blue sea."

Tops Diner was busy and warm, but beyond steamed glass the morning was dank as a basement and just as gloomy, fog tumbling in wide arcs. See a lawyer, people told him. Find out about your rights. But lawyers, like doctors, in Frankie's opinion, were mostly trouble-makers and vultures. "Stick up for yourself, Frankie," his Aunt Rosa would say. "Don't let her walk all over you. You give people like that an inch and you know what they do? They do you dirt, that's what." She never used Connie's name, only some Polish word that sounded like cockroach. "That cockroach, she don't care. You got a lemon, Frankie." Rosa had hung the framed photograph of his daughter Tracy, at two years old, behind her chair because, she said, she didn't want to spend the livelong day crying over spilt milk.

She'd have a fit, seeing him, he was thinking. Might run away again and not tell him where. Then what? But he saw himself driving south, past Squaw Bay and the sign that told people they were half-way between the Equator and the North Pole, saw himself heading down highways—first only two lanes, then three, then four. He saw Connie's gray eyes snap awake at the door. She'd light a cigarette in the kitchen first thing and consider, her eyes going sleepy again. He heard himself saying, "Con. How're you?" And she, sulking, or maybe just pretending, would say, "OK. You?" And he'd say, "Con—" and she, taking a deep drag, considering, dangling a terry cloth slipper from one foot, her ankle tiny and white and gleaming, the purple veins showing through like mesh, and him just sitting there like a jerk, afraid the least little word might throw everything off, and so saying nothing, just sitting there, feeling the blood zip around inside him, watching that slipper dangling like some invitation she wasn't quite sure yet she wanted to make, her pink bathrobe too, sliding open just a little, just enough, and telling him *maybe*.

Maybe what? Maybe they could all come back here? No. She'd been gone over three months. At first he'd thought, let her get it out of her system. She'll come back if you don't bug her. He remembered the complaints. Their place was junky, too strung out; the bathroom was down the hall and they had to share it with a Jesus freak who never flushed. Their car was crummy; so was the town and everything in it. They'd never get away, never make the break, never get a break. When she drank too much, she'd start dancing by herself to an old Janis

Joplin album, snapping her frizzy hair back and forth so that he worried she might crack her neck.

"What do you want, Con? What should I do?"

"I don't know what I want! And you. You're always running over there. Always at her beck and call. What about that Vince? Let him come up here and take care of her. She's his mother, not yours. I can't believe what a pushover you are, Frankie. You gotta choose. I'm warning you."

In the end, she'd done the choosing. It was the night Rosa called the ambulance. When the crew came into her house—she had left the door unlocked for them—she was lying in bed, all dressed and ready to go. She kept her eyes shut, complaining of weakness, and the two men had to get over two hundred and forty pounds of dead weight onto the stretcher. In the emergency room, the doctor couldn't find anything wrong. He wanted to know why she'd called the ambulance. "I'm lonesome," Rosa had said. "I don't want to live alone no more. I can't get used to the house, empty like that. I get scared."

According to Rosa, the doctor had given her a good bawling out, saying she wasn't the only widow in town and that she'd just have to get used to it. This got Rosa going. The doctor called Frankie and told him to come and get Rosa and take her home. He stayed the night, sleeping in his old room. The next day Connie and Tracy were gone. So was the Pontiac and nearly all Connie's clothes. A note scrawled on the back of an envelope lay on the sticky kitchen table. *You're a pushover*, she'd written.

Frankie finished the coffee and decided. Go. Who knows? He might even find some job down there. A whole new life. He left a dollar bill under the saucer for Angie and wondered if people who were dying felt that way about each and every thing they did, saying to themselves: this is the last time; so much for that. The thought was a punch.

Outside the diner a newspaper dispenser framed headlines about the old Jimmy Hoffa case. Detroit, the murder capital of the U.S.A., he was thinking. Connie and Tracy were in Detroit. Everything here is crummy, she'd said. But now they were there. Frankie stopped. The damp air smelled of fish and chemicals from the wallboard factory on the bay. Across the street, red, white, and blue plastic drooped over a

row of large-sized used cars. Their windshields were covered with
white numbers crossed out for other white numbers. A depression,
people were saying. No jobs. But how could it be the town? Everything'd been OK. For a while. It must be him. He didn't measure up.
That's what was crummy. That's what she'd been telling him all the
time. Who was he trying to kid?

He turned the heater on full blast in his pickup, then snapped on
his portable tape player. *Tosca.* Sherrill Milnes. Luciano Pavarotti.
Janet Baker. At home he listened to his father's old records. Tapes
were for the truck and for work. He turned north, toward the plant.

Frankie bumped down a gravel road into the quarry and parked at
the end of a row of pickups and four-wheel-drives. Jack Fitzgerald was
following him in his Bronco. Above the fog, breaking now, clouds
were packed in tight pearl clouds, soot clouds. Yellow-gray smoke
from six stacks tilted inland, tangling with the fog. It was his habit to
check the tilt of smoke to see if the wind was offshore or off the lake.
Same with the sky. One day might be all gold and blue, the sun sliding
over the quarry like butter melting, the next, no sun to speak of and
the light going green, like river water, and everything in that tornado
haze glowing, the edges of the trucks and the big shovel, the roof of
the shack and the crusher, the chalky streaks in the quarry face, the
fringe of scrub on top, even his own hands. Everything would go still
then, so that you were almost scared to breathe. There were times
when he felt like throwing himself in the dust and waiting for whatever had to happen.

"Frankie," Jack said. He was thin, sinking inward, his face gray as
his work shirt, jacket, and pants. He wore a gray, billed cap. When he
spoke, he looked at the dirt. "You know they're talking layoffs."

"I heard."

"Sometimes it don't mean nothin', but you never know."

Frankie checked his wristwatch, and then Jack's gray hand was
wrapped tight around Frankie's forearm.

"You know I could kick tomorrow with these lungs of mine. You
know that, hey Frankie?"

The fingers tightened. Frankie wanted to pull away.

"So I told them, I said, if worse comes to worse, let that Frankie stay on instead a me. Let the young who need it work, I said. I don't need no more money for the little time I got left."

"That's all right, Jackie—"

"But they say rules is rules. They can't lay off a union rep, they say. Cripes, I says. You guys are supposed to be helpin', not screwin' things up. That Frankie kin use the money, I says. And Pete, that son of a gun, he says, then maybe he shoulda got himself elected union rep. I told him, I says, Frankie don't operate like that. I told them. But what can you do?"

"I don't know." Frankie pulled forward. The grip loosened but not all the way, and Frankie had to stop again.

"I just want to say one thing, Frankie. You hang on now. You know what I mean?" He swatted his chest. "It won't be long." Tin banged on the roof of the shack that was the office.

"Don't talk like that," Frankie said. "You don't know."

Jack spat in the dust. "I don't know is right." Wind tugged at a rusty shrub of pigweed. Dirt scattered.

Frankie climbed up into his fifty-ton Euclid, the tires of which, he figured, were as high as a Chevrolet tipped upward and balanced on one bumper. He lodged his tape player on the extra seat, started up, and checked his gauges. The shovel was working the northeast section of the quarry, scooping up slabs and chunks of limestone blasted away from the quarry wall. This blasting made the quarry floor grow a little each year, and he sometimes speculated on all the things that could now fit down there—a subdivision, maybe fifty or so bars, a couple of drive-in movies. When the blasting crew went to work, people in town said it sounded just like bombs going off or like jets from the SAC base breaking the sound barrier, but as far as Frankie knew, no one ever complained. Work was work.

He followed Jack's truck, already nearing the shovel. The Euclid handled like a Caddy, not that he'd ever driven one so as to really know. He felt it must be similar. Everything under and around him, power brakes, steering, the works. He just floated along, bouncing forward on a lake of dust. All the truck needed was a brain and a pair of eyes, and hands not necessarily human. That would come, he figured. Computerized trucks running on a circular track, maybe. Or else trucks run by robots. The thought always screwed him up for a while. He envied Jack, bad lungs and all, who'd have his pension in a year or so. It didn't pay to think too much about it. And when you came right down to it, most jobs were probably pretty much the same. Except, maybe, for those people who got to sing.

Don't get moody, buddy, he told himself. Don't get nutsy so early. That was the thing. Too much time to think, driving around in a circle for eight hours. That's why the Brothers Bar down the road from the plant did such a knock-out business. He wondered if bus drivers or long-distance truckers had the same problem. He passed two ponds he liked to look at. One had a few dusty cattails. The sheets of water were dark, almost black, and wrinkled by the wind.

Jack pulled away from the shovel, and Frankie edged in parallel to it and just a bit ahead, then set the brake and idled. In a moment the bump came above and behind him, making the truck jounce a little. The shovel operator gave a blast on his horn, and Frankie took his place in the caravan of lime-green Euclids heading for the crusher.

He pressed the rewind, then the forward button on the tape player, and saw Angelotti rushing from hot sunlight into the cool damp of a church. Angelotti on the run, breathing hard, checking things out all around him. He sees a figure and stops, but it's only a shadow. *Ah!* he cries, *Final-men-te! Nel terror mio stolto vedea cef-fi di birro in o-gni vol-to.* Frankie closed his eyes at Angelotti's bass C-sharps and felt a quickening pleasure that was almost terror. He wanted to shout, to jump right out of the cab. Then booming chords, loud sharps and flats, smashed downward, diminishing to soft staccatos. He could hear the Euclid's engine grinding away. People who sang like that weren't human, he believed. Maybe angels. Maybe something else. But definitely not human.

The crusher was on the fritz. There was a big lineup. "Jam!" he heard, rolling down his window. That was all right—just a big mouth stuffed too full to chew or swallow. He didn't envy the guys who had to poke around in that steel jaw. They could have that job. He turned up his music and leaned back. Other guys, he knew, were flipping open magazines. One kid even worked on correspondence courses—carpentry, wiring, masonry—during stalls. He'd told Frankie he was getting married and wanted to build his own house in the country.

When he talked about these plans, Frankie knew he was looking at something the rest of them couldn't see.

"Hey, Caruso!" Rabbit Latinsky yelled. Standing in dust to the left of the line of trucks, Latinsky, a short, beer-bellied man, threw his head back, made stiff branches of his arms, the fingers curled as if paralyzed, and yowled and yodeled and made falsetto sweeps up and down a crazy scale. Rabbit Latinsky was giving Frankie Stepanski the business. Frankie waved at him. Everybody knew how Frankie couldn't stay away from water towers, oil storage tanks, railroad bridges, whatever. And they paid his court fees and fines for trespassing. Latinsky bowed in four directions to hoots and catcalls, and ran for his truck. The line was rolling.

Shovel. Crusher. Shovel. Again, again, again. Scarpia prays to ensnare Tosca. Bars of sunlight broke through a vent in the clouds, and yellow-gray smoke tilted eastward. Frankie stopped the tape. Leave right after work, he was thinking. Clothes didn't matter, and money he could get. One Euclid stopped, then another and another. Frankie slammed on his brakes just in time. Jack stuck his head out his window. "Hey, Frankie! You see that?" Two deer, tipping back and forth like rocking horses, were heading for the ponds. Frankie rolled down his window to see them better. They'd talk about it for days, he knew. Nobody could figure out how the heck deer got down into the quarry and out again. The shovel operator gave two sharp blasts on his horn and the caravan started up again.

"Let me buy you a drink," Jack said, after work. "To celebrate." Frankie hadn't gotten a layoff slip.

"I gotta get going. But thanks," Frankie said.

The kid who wanted to build a house in the country passed them, carrying a stack of books and his lunch pail.

Jack turned away and spat. "Tough break," he said. "Works ass-backwards, if you ask me."

"I'll see you, Jackie."

"Tomorrow. If you're lucky."

No, Frankie thought.

At the top of the road leading from the quarry, Frankie braked, and the compass on his dash bobbed between east and southeast. Ahead of him was the plant—gray conveyer chutes, whited-out windows, gray kilns and stacks. The whole place looked crusted over and gray-green, like something hauled up out of the lake. He turned north, onto a gravel road leading out of the plant area and into a no-man's-land of swamp cedar, inlets, and narrow sand beaches.

At a faded sign nailed to a tree—Misery Bay Boat and Tackle Rental—Frankie turned into a rutted lane curving through swamp cedar. The road gave out on a patch of grass broken by clumps of birch. Boats lay piled on the beach. A wooden mallard on a post paddled its wings in the wind. A woman came out of the cottage and stood waiting in the yard.

"You want a motor?" she said, when he was close enough.

Frankie said no, and the woman walked to an aluminum shed for the cushion and oars. She was wearing baggy pants, boots, and a bulky sweater. Her hair, as always, was hidden under the wool cap she wore winter and summer. Frankie had never seen her hair and often wondered about it. He thought he might like to see it one time. Everything about her was a mystery to him. People said she was part Chippewa. Her husband, they said, a Bartuszewski, ran off years ago, leaving her the cottage, the boats, and six dilapidated cabins in the woods. She called herself Florence Bartow and drove a pickup whenever she went into town, which was seldom. "What the heck do you do out here winters?" Frankie once asked her. She hadn't answered. Sometimes she wouldn't talk at all, just motion to this or that boat and go back to her cottage. "Crazy Indian," people said. "No wonder that Bartuszewski took off like a bat. She probably slammed him around like she slams those boats of hers." When she took money—never checks—she stuffed it into whatever pocket was handy and never made change. It was Florence Bartow who'd told him about the name of the bay.

"When they got sick, they came out here to die."

"Who did?"

"Indians."

She wouldn't tell him any more, even though he'd asked.

Out on the lake the aluminum boat swung around the anchor, and Frankie faced open water. He made a few casts, his line singing in the wind, then let the daredevil drag bottom. If he left that minute, he'd get to her apartment sometime in the middle of the night. If he left at eleven, he'd get there before she went to work in the morning. What

kind of fit would she have then? If he'd gone right after breakfast, he'd
be there by now. The thought didn't stir him. He was flat as the lake.

Frankie heard distant humming, and then the air filled with butterflies, thousands of monarchs. He stuck his arm straight up. The cloud
shifted slightly, pouring over it. Soon the blur of color became a
smudge against the lighter gray of sky. He watched it until he couldn't
see anything. The water went a darker green. The wind grew sharp.
He reeled in.

"They do that every year," Florence Bartow said, when he brought
in the boat. Together they hauled it up onto the stony strip of beach.
She threw the anchor on the grass. "I watch for them," she said.
Frankie looked at the horizon, the wall of storm cloud there. He
started worrying about the butterflies, then about something else.
Everything seemed to be moving except the two of them. He wanted
to ask if she might consider taking off that wool cap, for just a second.
He had a notion, he wanted to tell her, that her hair must be something. But then he was getting out his wallet. Florence Bartow took
the money and headed for her cottage.

Under the cedars it was already night. A light went on in the cottage, and Frankie started up the truck. You don't know what you
want, he told himself. That's for damn sure.

He circled the town like a high-school kid, the compass tipping
south, then west, then north. He passed the road sign that gave the dis-
tances from that point to Detroit, the Moon, and Venus. Not far away
were several oil storage tanks and a water tower. He eyed these but
kept going. Downtown, the one movie theater was showing Bronson
in *Death Wish*. He didn't think he'd care for it. He passed Rosa's
house and imagined her sprawled in her easy chair before the TV,
watching "The Joker's Wild" and waiting for him to get home and
bring in the mail. By now she might have eaten her Meals-on-Wheels
dinner left over from lunch, and she'd be on her second pack of cigarettes. He slowed, but then Connie was saying in her small voice,
You're a pushover, Frankie. You're such a jerk. He stepped on the gas,
hit a deep pothole, and his fishing gear made a racket in the back. The
compass bobbed north again. He thought of picking up a bottle and
heading back out to Misery Bay, but his nerve failed him. He wound
up at the Brothers.

A plastic bag of water with something swimming in it sat on the bar between a man and a woman Frankie regarded as low-lifers. The man was putting on a show for anyone who'd watch.

"Yuk!" the barmaid said. She was looking closely at the bag.

"What *are* those?"

"You got me," the man said. "I don' know nothin' 'bout them. We just liketa buy somethin' different. We come inta town, cash our checks, and buy somethin' different every time." The string-haired girl next to him—wife or daughter or girlfriend, Frankie couldn't tell—pushed a coloring book and a box of crayons away from her Coke. Both the man and the girl were chain-smoking.

"Tire-track eels!" The barmaid dropped the small tag attached to the neck of the bag. "Yuk!"

Two brown eels, not much bigger than pike minnows, Frankie figured, turned circles in a few inches of water, their long narrow fins rippling. It made him sick to watch them, but not because they were ugly.

"There's only one more thing I want," the man boomed over the string-haired girl's head.

The barmaid didn't take him up on it. The string-haired girl spoke quietly. "What's that? A monkey?"

"You still guessin'?"

"What?"

The man swiveled toward the barmaid. "A .44 caliber machine gun. I got the other kinds. Now I want me one a those."

"Well, we sure as heck don't sell none of those here." The barmaid giggled, gave the eels one more wary look, and went to the opposite end of the bar.

The man doled out some coins and pushed them near his empty shot glass. "So long, sweetheart!" he hollered at the barmaid. They walked past Frankie, the man dangling the bag of eels, the girl cradling her coloring book and crayons. Frankie imagined the guy dropping the bag somewhere, at another bar maybe, the water spilling out everywhere, men laughing, the eels flopping around. Or maybe they'd be left on a car seat to freeze solid as hamburger, or flushed down the toilet, or dumped into some ditch.

"Hey!" Frankie shouted.

The man stopped at the door and pulled away from the girl. Somebody touched Frankie's shoulder.

"You callin' me, kiddo?"

Frankie stood. "I want to buy them eels off you."

"Buy your goddam own."

Somebody laughed. Frankie walked toward the man. His neck and ears were going hot. It wouldn't be a fair fight, unless the guy had a knife. Or a gun. He held out his hand. "Let me see them."

"Hey. What is this?"

Frankie heard the whine of fear under the words. He had the guy's number. He went closer. "I want to buy them off you for my aunt. I've been looking for that kind."

"You crack me up," the man said. "Get your big ass over to Woolworth's and buy your own."

"I'll give you twenty bucks."

"What's the joke?" The man smirked. "What's the punch line?" He nudged the girl, who was staring at the floor.

Frankie wanted to grab the guy and slam him, eels and all, but he made himself consider the man's cheap plastic jacket.

"Maybe we kin jack him up to fifty, hey?" the man said. "What d'you say, big boy? What about youse guys?" he yelled toward the bar. "These eels are goin' to the highest bidder." He dangled the bag before Frankie.

Frankie pulled out two tens from his wallet. The man wiped his mouth. The girl's eyes urged him to take the money, but he undid the neck of the bag and spilled out half the water. The eels thrashed. "You want 'em, you better step on it!" Frankie took out a five.

"This is fun," the man said over his shoulder to the girl, and Frankie grabbed his arm, twisting it until he could yank away the bag, all the while pushing the guy toward the door. The girl was holding it open, and this struck Frankie as a hell of a note. But the guy went limp all of a sudden, and Frankie knew the fight was over. At the door he got the crushed money into the girl's hands. Her face was a blotchy white. She dropped her coloring book.

"Sure!" the man whined. "A real tough mother!" He let the girl pull him away.

Frankie put the coloring book on the table nearest the door. It was brand-new, with a palomino horse on the cover. Someone handed him his wallet, but he was thinking of that golden horse rearing up, its white mane and tail flaring out, and he banged his fist against the table, making the ashtray and salt and pepper shakers jump.

"Hell of a catch, Frankie!"

"Hey Frankie, you better watch out for the game warden. They look undersize to me!"

Someone started a story that had nothing to do with anything, as far as Frankie could tell, but he listened to take his mind off the eels, now swimming alongside his beer glass.

"—and that Moltke got so damn drunk, he was crying to himself in his car, crying himself sick. What's the matter with you? we said. What the heck you crying for? Somebody stole my wheel! he said, and kept up the crying. What wheel? we said. An' we walked all around his car. All the wheels are here, we told him. My steering wheel! Moltke bawled. Somebody took my steering wheel and I can't drive! You crazy fool, we said. You're sitting in the backseat! *Hoo-whoo!*"

Some of the men were wiping their eyes. Frankie finally had to laugh too.

"It takes all kinds, don't it?" the storyteller said.

"Frankie," Rosa said, "where the heck you been so darn long?" She shifted in her recliner and took the mail he left on her TV tray. The tray was piled high with medicine, Kleenex, mints, cigarettes, and magazines. A fingernail file fell to the rug. He picked it up and stuck it in her *TV Guide*.

"Fishing."

"I don't see no fish."

He raised the bag of eels. Rosa looked up from the mail. "Oh, for cripes sake. What the heck is that?"

"Eels. I bought them off a guy."

"Frankie, don't go bringing that kind of stuff home. Get rid of them. I don't want those things in here."

He took the eels into the kitchen and looked for something to put them in.

"Frankie?" Rosa called over the sound of screeching birds on TV. "I don't want them in the kitchen!"

"OK, OK," he yelled back, and took a stainless steel pan from the set Rosa had inherited from Frankie's mother. Jesus in Heaven, what if it's salt water? he thought. He opened the bag and tasted the water. No. He put the eels in the kettle, gave them more water, and took them into his bedroom. When he went back into the living room, Rosa was through looking at the mail.

"That Vince," she said. "He don't write."

"He will."

"Don't you go sticking up for him, Frankie. How long does a letter take? He could write to say where he is. But no. He don't write. He don't even call. Who knows what happened."

"Can I turn this down?" Frankie went to the TV, where thousands of birds were flying low over some lake. They gave him a headache. *I thought I'd drive down to Detroit,* he practiced. *See Connie and Tracy. Maybe I could try and look up Vince.*

"I thought—" he began.

"Turn it off." Rosa waved her cigarette. "I only have it on for the noise when no one's here. It's too darn quiet."

He turned down the sound but left the picture. Outside, tractor-trailers roared by, making the windows shake, while on TV birds skimmed down on the lake in silence and folded their wings almost in unison. They covered every inch of the lake. *Listen,* he practiced, *Why don't we—you and—* He went back to the couch, the thought unformed.

"They used to have that Purple Gang down there," Rosa was saying. "Who knows what they got now." Her smooth, large face was shiny with tears.

"Vince is OK. He'll give you a call one of these days." At his father's funeral, Vince had gone around telling everyone he was in insurance, but the name of the company rang no bells. He was dressed to kill and made a point of kissing all the women, young and old, at the funeral parlor. Frankie had wanted to punch him out.

"You always stick up for him, Frankie." Rosa went for her Kleenex. On TV the birds were airborne again. They reminded Frankie of the butterflies, flying all together like that. Now they blotted out the sky.

Rosa watched the silent birds flickering across the screen for a moment, then fixed the blanket over her legs. "You know that Mrs. Vernie?" Twin gray threads of smoke from her cigarette tangled and looped, rising to the ceiling. The air in the room stung Frankie's eyes.

"The one that just died?"

"The family gave her hairdresser a real big tip for fixing her hair so nice. And you know what?"

"What?"

"She had a closed casket." Rosa stared at the wall above the birds. Ash fell to the rug. "I want one, too. You make sure, Frankie. I don't want nobody looking at me like that."

Oh, Christ, Frankie said to himself. To Rosa, he said. "Don't talk like that, hey?"

She wouldn't look at him now. The tears kept coming and she made no motion to stop them. "You have to," she said.

"You hungry? Did you have anything for supper?"

Rosa took a long time to answer. "Today was macaroni and cheese. You could maybe warm the second one up for yourself if you want."

"Let's split it."

"Maybe just a little bit," she finally said.

In the kitchen he fought the same urge to take off as he'd had at the funeral parlor the night he arranged for his uncle's funeral. It was after eleven when he'd gotten there, yet the undertaker was wearing white shoes, gray trousers, and a navy blazer with brass buttons. He flicked on lights as they went down carpeted flights of stairs and through a carpeted hallway leading to a windowless room with pink walls, red carpeting, and shiny open caskets resting on trestles. Frankie was aware of the quiet, then the low hum of fluorescent lighting, and nearly balked, but the undertaker stepped forward, all business and fast talk. He reminded Frankie of a used-car salesman, as he pointed out the advantages and disadvantages of a few caskets, hinting at the dangers of water seepage in the cheaper models. "Now this one," he told Frankie, standing before a bronze-tone casket with puffs of pink lining, "this you don't have to be ashamed of. This is first-class. And who wants to cut corners at a time like this, hey?" Frankie knew he was being taken for a ride, but he didn't care. He just wanted out. That brown one would be OK, he said. "You're a dying breed," the undertaker told him, then had to laugh. He hustled Frankie out, flicking off lights behind them as they climbed the stairs, and that's when he'd wanted to run.

He turned off the microwave he'd gotten Rosa for Christmas and thought of Moltke bawling in the backseat of his car. It was funny, you had to admit, but *Jesus*.

On TV Leonard Bernstein was conducting an orchestra. Hair hung over his brow; his face was wet. His eyes were closed, and he almost seemed to be crying. The camera cut to a close-up of a violinist. His eyes were closed, too, his eyebrows raised as if he were fighting off pain. The camera went back to Bernstein, whose eyes now were open. Wherever he pointed with his stick, Frankie thought, people went through hell. Not all, though. Some faces might have been chunks of limestone. He turned up the volume a fraction—the piece slow, weird. Any minute now Rosa would have fits. He glanced at her. She was taking small jabs at the macaroni and cheese, but not eating any of it. He looked at the orchestra again.

"Frankie," Rosa said. "What kind of music is that? I don't like it."

He turned off the sound and watched Bernstein's face.

"Frankie, you know, I was thinking. Maybe I should go into that Providence House." She stopped jabbing at the macaroni.

On the couch he sipped his can of beer and considered. At the nursing home there would be people to take care of her. She wouldn't be alone so much during the day. She might make a few friends. And he— He sipped more beer. It could have been summertime and ninety degrees, the way he was sweating. "You don't want to do that," he said, his heart gearing up.

She put her plate and fork on the TV tray, where it slid, lodged against something, stayed. She covered her eyes with one hand. "No," she said.

Frankie sighed. In the space of an instant he'd pried off the storm windows, aired out the house, painted, washed cupboards, and bought a complete new set of living room furniture. Tracy was there, playing with toys on a thick new rug. Ah, he was a selfish bastard.

"Aunt Rosa, what's the matter?" She was massaging her temples, her eyebrows raised like the violinist's.

"My head hurts."

"How does it hurt?"

"It just hurts."

"You want some aspirin?"

"It's not that."

"What then?"

"My scalp is all cracking."

"How come?"

"I don't know. Maybe from not washing my hair enough."

"So when did you wash it last?"

"Oh, that Mrs. Schiemke sometimes comes and I ask her, but—"

She was crying again, to herself. The worst kind of crying, in his book. On TV Bernstein was smiling a little. And the violinist, too, smiling like a baby. Frankie figured they'd pulled through the bad spot.

In the kitchen he cleared glasses and silverware and aluminum tins from the sink, ran warm water in a plastic dishpan and found the shampoo. Then he helped Rosa out of her chair and walked her to the kitchen, the folds of her big upper arm loose in his grasp. She bent slowly, wheezing, over the sink, and he scooped warm water over stiff curls that looked like woodwork. They fell apart at once. Rosa flinched. "Shush," he said, shampooing the wet gray tufts against the enflamed scalp. He worked the shampoo in as gently as he could, and felt under his big hands the old bones, the loose, cracked skin. He saw his uncle in the coffin. His father. *Jesus*, he wanted to yell, and rubbed too hard. Her head swerved from his hands. She gasped. "Wait," he said, getting the hair over the pan again. "You know what? I heard this good story today. When we get done, I'll tell you. Maybe you knew the guy."

"What guy?"

"Wait. I'm almost finished. I'll tell you."

"Frankie—" She sniffed. "You're OK. You know that? Don't ever let anybody tell you different."

"Sure," he said. She was crying again.

He couldn't sleep. The day played itself back like a scratched record, sticking here, jumping there. A car went by, then a tractor-trailer, then a car again. His clock on the nightstand ticked away. A statue of St. Joseph on the bureau gave off faint light. He watched this light go dimmer and dimmer. He thought he could hear the eels flipping around in their pan under the statue and started worrying about what they ate. Traffic picked up. Eels, for Chrissake. On top of everything else, eels. They'd make jokes about it at the Brothers. He held his wristwatch to the street light falling between the shade and windowsill. Almost six. Close enough. He put on his work pants, his heavy socks and boots, his work shirt.

Hand over hand he climbed steel rungs wet with frost. The oil tank, inches from his face, breathed cold. At the top he stepped back from the edge, its pull. Behind him, the dark of jack pine woods. Above, all black. But columns of broken light lay over the river; and in the east, streaks of daylight. Connie's pink bathrobe, he was thinking, with those red threads running through the washed-out material. Wind off the lake carried the wallboard factory's stink in low white clouds. He heard descending chords, then eighth notes, a soft staccato. Raising his head, he sang, *Re-con-di-ta ar-mo-ni-a*, forming D then F, eighth and quarter notes, then the melancholy, sustained E, *di-bel-lez-ze di-ver-se!* . . . The high G was ahead of him, waiting, and he swung toward it *È bru-na, Flo-ri-a, l'ar dente aman-te mi—a—*

Headlights bobbed as a truck hit the railroad tracks. A spotlight picked him out. "Hey, Caruso!" Rabbit Latinsky yelled. "Hey! Frank-ee!" Other trucks pulled off the road and parked alongside Rabbit Latinsky's pickup—men on their way to work. His singing was an event, he knew, like smelt running in the river, and just as unpredictable. But Frankie was only half-aware of the guys. He was looking at Florence Bartow standing on her stony beach at Misery Bay, her black hair flying, and behind her, the lake all choppy and green. *Ah!* he sang, *il mio sol pen-sier sei tu! To—ósca sei tu!* He held onto the final high E for as long as he could. Horns were blasting away, as at band concerts, and other spotlights picked him out. Guys were hollering Bravo! and Whoo! and More, Frankie, more! A state police cruiser bounced over the railroad tracks, its flashers on, but Frankie was looking out over the flat town, at the widening light above the lake, and thinking that just because he hadn't gone to Detroit didn't mean he'd never go. And if things didn't pan out in Detroit— He saw Florence Bartow in her wool cap, carrying oars and flotation cushions. *Who could tell?* it hit him. Who could tell what the heck might happen when a person still had some time left. That was the thing right there. A person shouldn't lose sight of *that.* Below him everyone went still, and he heard the muted fanfare, the tambourine chink of sheep bells and the shepherd boy calling and church bells striking the Angelus and the rising eighth notes and quickening, falling sixteenths, and then he was singing again, creating, in his imperfect tenor, Cavaradossi's perfect sorrow.

a novella

KAHUNA

Try, the old priest told himself. It scared him, this putting off and putting off. Need boiling over; the spirit needy, but the flesh stymied somehow, seized up. The mental groping each morning, casting about for coherence, certainty, a starting point, then shrinking back, giving up and going out to the *lanai* to look at the ocean, below in the distance, silver in afternoon light. Then before he knew it, another sunset. In the evening, sometimes, he forced himself to stay in his study for a few hours, as now, but that was often worse—the worry, the quiet, the dark all around, the isolated house holding it. He was half-certain Tomas Koe must be haunting him, for what was any haunting, maybe, but the emanations of a guilty conscience. If he were a drinker, he'd be a goner by now. As it was, he could only take his various medications and go to sleep finally, hoping not to dream. The thing was, he told himself, not to worry about how much time—months!—he'd already squandered in this way, after all the work finding the right house, the necessary quiet and isolation. The thing was not to scare himself thinking how little time he had left and just begin.

But he pushed back his chair, the elegant fountain pen still in hand—a Mont Blanc pen his well-to-do brother Walt had sent him as a retirement gift. The priest had written the family in Wisconsin that he'd be staying on in Hawaii to do some writing he'd been putting off. He didn't mention, of course, that after over forty years in the Islands he could no more think of going back there for good than flying to the moon. This was his home, for better or worse, even if he'd made such a mess of things and now felt in permanent exile from his former parish in the village of Pahoa on the other side of the island. Nor had his words to the family conveyed anything of the urgency he felt about the writing he must do. Walt had written back, jokingly referring to his memoirs, and sending the extravagant gift. They were, however, threatening to visit, and that worried him—the loss of time it would mean, but above all they'd see how he was living, so isolated in an arid, unpopulated section overlooking the Pacific. See that and worry, maybe start agitating. He was living like one of the desert Fathers, the old priest sometimes thought, but lacking their sanctity and great talents. Or like a penitent hermit—El Greco's St. Peter weeping and praying in his cave. But those comparisons were far too flattering.

He glanced at his wristwatch on the desk, hoping it might be late enough to justify calling it quits, but it was only 9:20. He wondered what his successor, Father Huntly, was doing right then at Our Lady of Sorrows. Sitting on the *lanai,* sipping some drink and trying to figure out how to bring in more money and more parishioners? A real go-getter, the old priest had known right away—even though so young, impossibly young. Just a kid running about in Levi's and T-shirts half the time. And Kani, the old priest's friend and current housekeeper, had told him she'd heard Father Huntly was going full speed ahead on several gambling projects, of all things—Bingo Nite! and Million Dollar Adventure raffles, and something new called Paradise Ventures. Remembering this caused a rush of uncharitable thoughts, but he couldn't help it. They were scraping the bottom of the barrel! In the old days Father Huntly would have been counseled out in no time. Given the bum's rush.

Oh, jealous. That was for sure. And above all, pained that this hot-shot was to be his confidant, and confessor, really, for what he had to write would be a confession. And a warning. Early in his retirement he'd hoped Father Huntly might surprise him with a visit; they'd talk, there'd be some warmth, some spark, and he could say what had to be said, tell the entire story. But that hadn't happened, and shame kept the old priest from returning to the Pahoa rectory. Shame, pride, and fear of muddling it all if he tried to talk, he was so addled at times.

Something fell in the house. A heavy bump, then only wind humming through the screens. The old priest's heart lurched into its ragged trotting pace. *What*. The cat? Maybe just the wind knocking something down? But he knew if he went out into the other rooms and turned on the lights, he'd find everything in place. Nothing tipped over. It happened too often, just this way. Something—a bump or crash, then nothing. The noise concentrating him to a fine, burning point of attention, then the stillness eventually releasing him into his chaotic, exhausting thoughts.

"Tomas?" he said. "If you're spooking around here— I know this is your great-grandfather's old stomping grounds, the *heiau* temple at Kawaihai and all . . . We have to forgive, Tomas. That's the thing. And here I thought you had!"

Oh he was nuts! Nutsy-cuckoo. He laughed aloud, and this gave him enough courage to draw back the scattering thoughts. Father Huntly impossibly young. Young stock! And for that reason, all the more—dangerous.

The thought, chilling, jolted him just as the strange sound had. He leaned toward the blank sheet of paper, and the pen, touching it, hurriedly set off across its white expanse, leaving in its wake a blue string of wobbly writing.

By now you may have heard a few rumors, Father Huntly. How I've gone round the bend, as they say, and am living with a woman companion here on the Kona side. A few parishioners have kindly let me in on the "talk." If it'll help avoid scandal, just go ahead and say, Oh, he's a little off, poor soul. But the truth is, with my medications I'm really OK, though they do make me a little goofy at times, and as for Kani—

The priest's pen made a long slash and skidded into clear territory.

My Dear Father Huntly: You know why I retired. Bad health. That's partially the case, but what you don't know is that I was asked to step down, give up parish duties, because, they said, I was getting dangerously close to preaching heresy. Heresy. The word still packs a wallop, doesn't it? They generously blamed my "confused" thinking on the several minor strokes I suffered in recent years. I didn't argue—too little time left for that. The thing is, what I'd come round to in my thinking, and sermons eventually, is that doubt goes hand in hand with humility; whereas blind faith can seduce us into terrible pride and arrogance. Think of the Crusaders, for example, or that chaplain blessing the men and the plane that dropped the bombs on Hiroshima and Nagasaki. Or even, come to think of it, those deeply earnest people now bombing abortion clinics and tormenting the unfortunate women going there to have abortions.

What I'm getting at here is the question of—the problem of—doubt and faith. Yes. That's what my sermons were about at the end—whether doubt may be better than "wrong-headed" faith. Of course I probably put it badly, being on medication and all, and probably wound up causing a lot of—problems. If so, I'm very sorry. And I can see why the powers-that-be wanted to put me out to pasture. But what I have to tell you is how I came to that "heresy." It's so important, Father Huntly, that you know this, and not just pick up rumors here and there having to do with me and Tomas Koe. The thing is, I'm still trying to straighten all that out in my mind, the finer points, though the gist of it is all too clear. As pastor, I did damage, Father Huntly. A lot of damage. Our bishop doesn't know the half of it—what led to those mixed-up sermons of mine. What I'm really guilty of has little to do with "academic" points of theology, Father Huntly, and quibbles over word choice. No! What I'm to blame for is flesh and blood stuff, and all tangled up with a lot of pain, for several people, including myself. So what I need to do now, above all, is try and set it out straight so you'll understand the—dangers.

The pen wobbled to a stop. The old priest's hand was trembling. Amazed, he saw words on several pages, and he wasn't tired at all, just thirsty. And surprised.

—Tomas? Did you do this, or what?

His mind, released from memory, skittered to a new worry—what to do with his Mont Blanc pen, who should have it after he died? Kani didn't write much. Michael Koe, Tomas's son? In property rests all the problems of mankind. Who said that? Rousseau? Proudhon? Or did he just make it up?

In the kitchen he spoke to Francis, the gecko on the windowsill over the sink, who was eyeing the small insects slipping in through the screen and massing as close to the fluorescent light as they could get. Every so often Francis would unstick himself and dart out at them, consuming, the priest knew, great numbers. But still others would swarm in to the light. The cruelty of leaving the light on over the sink seemed equally balanced by the cruelty of depriving Francis of his nightly meal. The old priest checked his pill organizer, kept in the left-hand cupboard with the glasses. The plastic container reminded him of a dish for holding deviled eggs. In the space for Monday, all the pills were gone—the Inderal, the potassium supplement, the blood thinner, and the vitamins and garlic pills he got from the natural food store in Kamuela. He took vitamin A, made from pure fish oils, for his dry, flaking skin that never tanned but chipped off everywhere, giving his skin a bronze-freckled, mottled white and pink effect, something rather like the texture of a pointillist painting. Seeing all those pills waiting to be taken was comforting. Colorful beads promising him another day, and another, and—who knows?—maybe a few more after that. Enough, he hoped, to finish what he must do.

Wind off the Kohala range whistled in the screens. Kani's imitation *tapa* cloth curtains were damp. He slid the window halfway shut, causing Francis to hide behind the paper-towel holder. The time surprised him, after midnight.

"Enough gorging!" he told Francis and shut the window. A water bug, disturbed by the racket, sped across the floor. This creature, he knew, was probably still alive due to his intercession with Kani. He hated to kill anything quite that large, and each water bug, that a euphemism much nicer than cockroach, was as large as a fat Dromedary date. He was sometimes good at catching them in empty plastic containers and then releasing them outside, even though he knew they just came back in again. Kani, on the other hand, would smash them with whatever was handy, on those days she came in to clean. "Now I get you, eh?" she'd say. Then smash, bang—kettle, broom, her rubber thong. Or else she laid out strips of tape laden with boric acid. All for the best, he supposed. One couldn't be overrun. But this smashing and banging, these wiles exerted against lesser creatures disturbed him.

He turned off the kitchen light and in the few seconds of blindness saw the skinned body of a deer, marbled white and maroon, hanging from the oak in their front yard in Wisconsin. His hand jerked up to calm his heart. Every deer-hunting season his father had strung up his kill this way to signify, for anyone passing by on the macadam county road, his self-sufficiency and prowess. Later, when the priest's brothers had grown old enough to hunt, there'd be several deer strung up out front. For years this image would unexpectedly jolt him at odd moments at school, or while walking to the school bus stop, or before falling asleep. It would just be there, hanging motionless in the frozen air and glowing blue-white. Then would come shame and fear and anger, a jumble of emotions branding him as the soon-to-be prodigal. Now, frightened at what might be a premonition, he hurried back to his study and took up the pen, still warm to the touch.

When I first stepped off the boat some forty years ago, Father Huntly, I was excited and scared, but also eager to begin, just as you probably were, too. Hawaii hadn't been my first choice, though. From my seminary vantage point in the hills of southwestern Wisconsin, I regarded Hawaii as too tame, not enough of a challenge. I wanted—it was crazy!—the rigors of Indonesia. I had a large wall map of Southeast Asia tacked over my study desk, and the fragmented land masses against all that blue looked like the pieces of a puzzle, or like some delicate object that had fallen to the floor and shattered. The mottled gold of Sumatra and Java, Borneo and the Celebes flickered and beckoned. I was sure I was meant to live out my life there and come into some flowering. I still believe we all possess the same capacity for fruition as a plum tree, or a tiger lily—in a spiritual sense—but it's just not as obvious nor as genetically programmed. And in my case, though I'd missed out pretty much completely on any physical flowering, I desperately desired the spiritual.

After my Ordination, I was slated to go to Djakarta and from there travel east across the island of Java to the tiny isle of Madura, off the coast and about two hundred kilometers northwest of Bali. Those exotic words! It was all so strange. There I was, from hardy Midwestern stock, but an anomaly, bookish, heat-sensitive; fifteen minutes in direct sunlight and my face and arms went wild, flaring into a bumpy, painful rash. Imagine me, then, under my map's golden islands, composing a gracious note of thanks to my superior. But at the last minute my assignment was changed. A priest died in Hawaii, and I was thrown five thousand miles off course, as it were. I considered writing another note, of mild protest, but finally bought a new wall map and found a book in the library and meditated on the formation of the Hawaiian chain, their northwestern drift, and their eventual sinking back into the deep.

From the deck of the ship I watched the Big Island appear in blue haze and felt such excitement and joy, I might have been approaching Java after all. First, a cone of white floating above cloud—snow-clad Mauna Kea. Then as we drew closer, sheer cliffs and waterfalls—long filaments tumbling off those cliffs to white surf. And high above the impossibly blue water, green uplands with clouds all backlit by the sun and brilliant as opals. I imagined Adam first opening his eyes and shuddering at the light and color and forms. The surprise of it. I felt spangled with light! The railing seemed to melt from my hands, the deck fall away. I was nothing but light drawn to all that splendor. Something like emptiness pressed in everywhere, and for a second I thought I must be dying. But I felt no pain, nothing but bliss. It seemed I was looking outward from within a crust of ice shot through with sunlight. Then just as swiftly, terror was back. I could recognize nothing. Nothing familiar! All patterns and shifting light and vividness but nothing comprehended. Oh, Father Huntly, is this why kids take drugs today? I'm awfully out of touch, but I suspect it may be to experience something like that. To be free of ourselves for an instant, anyway. If so, I almost can't blame them. A sudden fall into Something Else. Is it possible that we might be in some evolutionary infancy as far as consciousness goes? Eyes to see yet seeing not, except for these rare glimpses? Even then we can hardly handle it. My father, for one, would have laughed at such a notion. Work hard and well, be honest, treat others fairly, and don't bother too much about all the rest. He was a good man, and one of the best dairy farmers in the state. He always changed his barn boots out on the porch, no matter how cold it might be. He scrubbed his hands and face and neck at the sink in a pantry off the kitchen, the water gushing hard all the while. He was the first to get electricity from the co-op; the first to install a bulk tank; the first to have a TV with a complicated antenna stuck atop something that looked like a narrow ladder to the stars. The TV was color, which meant it had a piece of cellophane tinted green, blue, and rose stuck over the picture tube. Once he took our mother for a weekend trip to the Dells, probably an anniversary, though I don't remember the details except that he wore his good suit, slate-blue, with a white cowboy shirt and black string tie held in place at the neck by silver steer horns. His reddish-black sideburns grew mossy along the broad, stony slant of face. It was the only overnight trip I can remember my father and mother taking. I used to watch him in church when a reading had to do with a stunning miracle—Christ restoring the blind man's sight with a bit of dust and spittle, or raising Lazarus, or later, after the Resurrection, appearing to others—that spooky business on the road to Emmaus, for example. I'd get chills, listening. Natural laws broken like so many toothpicks, and my father sitting there solemn and respectful, his eyes glazed, his big hands idle in his lap—hands scarred and distended at the knuckles from years of fiddling with busted equipment, barbed-wire fencing, motors and engines of all kinds, often in subzero weather when things had a natural inclination to give up and quit for good. The words were so familiar to him, maybe, they'd lost all content. Familiarity doesn't necessarily breed contempt but does seem to make things invisible—or at least commonplace; strips away their sheen, the iridescent strangeness. So what do we have now but young people flocking to the Reverend Moon, or to Indian gurus, or to the foothills of the Himalayas, where clotheslines of prayer flags strung across ravines flap eerily in mountain winds. What are they looking for? That strange-ness, I think. Whatever will shake all the molecules up, so that one is no longer the same—if only for a second. Maybe—who knows?—such leaps, however ephemeral, are to the evolution of consciousness what those astonishing leaps—fins into legs and arms, say—are to biological evolution.

Oh, I don't know beans about it, really, and shouldn't speculate. As for me, I made a frightening leap as well—from my parents' cool Luther-anism to Catholicism, and eventually to the priesthood, because these offered, at least, the possibility of Mystery. And for a startling, brilliant moment, the Big Island's Hamakua coast became both promise and the thing itself.

Imagine. There I was, hanging onto that railing for all I was worth. A young priest—plump, prematurely middle-aged, someone more at home in lamplit interiors, and colorless as certain mushrooms from feeding in libraries on the rich detritus of others' experiences and illuminations. Now, suddenly, to see that such experience could touch me. An epiphany? Or, you might argue, just thinking turned to mush by the chemistry of the moment, or the bad night's sleep the night before, or maybe it had to do with all those weeks at sea—nothing but clouds and unbroken space, then landfall at last and the blood going to town in relief, and the brain all tipsy, making the world too charged with light and significance—

The priest, pausing to rest his hand, saw a sudden, exciting connec-tion: cynicism and rationality. What was cynicism but rationality gone sour, and what was rationality but one of those new four-wheel-drive vehicles kids drove up and down mountain trails, or through lava fields, trying to reach inaccessible but glorious places. This image pleased him, the absurdity of the metaphor. Out of habit he jotted it down on a large index card for his sermon box, an old-time wooden cigar box he'd found in a Pahoa thrift shop.

But then he remembered he needn't prepare sermons anymore. That life was all done and gone, as his father used to say. He needn't do anything but somehow finish this letter to Father Huntly, and what a mess he was making of it—his brain tipsy on details! He imagined Father Huntly in an aloha shirt, a glass of cold papaya nectar beside him as he sat on the *lanai* at the rectory, impatiently scanning shaky script no credit to the exquisite pen, trying to discover its heart.

Enough digression! Enough wheel-spinning! Tomorrow, without fail, he must get to the story of Tomas Koe and his ten acres.

TWO

He couldn't sleep. All this dredging up of stuff had gotten him riled, and he was afraid of what he might dream in such a state. He wondered if Father Huntly appreciated the new cemetery and new community hall and parking lot. Probably not. Probably took them for granted, or else found fault and already had ideas for improvements of his own.

He felt a sudden longing for the plumeria-scented Puna nights, an ache of regret and nostalgia. He tried to picture the village as he'd first seen it, everything vivid in strong light. Our Lady of Sorrows, a clapboard church with some gingerbread fretwork, stood at one end of the village, the post office at the other. In between, strung along both sides of a road through sugarcane country, were simple frame buildings, shops and houses all topped with tin roofs—a tavern, a bakery, two or three dim grocery shops, a big cash and carry emporium selling everything from animal feeds and hardware to clothing, toys, and food. There was also a Buddhist temple constructed of wood, quite impressive with its oriental decorative woodwork. A tiny garage with one rusted gas pump stood on the outskirts of the village, surrounded by junked cars to be stripped for parts. Those who could afford to, painted their houses and shops; in bad times the wood was left to battle salt air and rain on its own and soon reverted to a mildewy, weathered gray. Red dust blew off the cane fields, and cane trucks scattered frayed and crushed stalks along the road. Tourists rarely stopped on their way to the scenic Black Sand Beach at Kalapana, or to the volcanic craters up on Mauna Loa. Yet the village wasn't without charm. Many of the small houses had, as front yards, their own luxurious anthurium beds shaded by tree ferns, and village women saw to it that the altar at Our Lady of Sorrows was never without vases of the heart-shaped blooms.

All this Father Huntly would experience for himself. But not the Akebono. Shouldn't he, in his letter, at least mention the movie theater that had been pulled down before Father Huntly arrived? It resembled a roller rink made of clapboard, and people had to sit on wooden folding chairs. Before showings of movies, the interior would be thoroughly sprayed with an insecticide—this sweetish-acrid scent lingering all through the movie. Ladies in long muumuus, with flowers in their hair, took tickets. Whole families went, carrying blankets and pillows, food, and children in their pajamas. He remembered the general weeping during *Gone With the Wind*. First somebody would start, then there'd be a whole slew of people sniffling, then it would be quiet for a bit until someone started the whole thing up again.

The old priest was wide awake now and annoyed with himself. There he was, musing over incidentals that had little to do with Tomas. He turned on the bedside lamp and put on his bathrobe. No, he thought. He was wrong. It had everything to do with Tomas. And with Tomas's children. Father Huntly must understand that Pahoa wasn't the end of the world, but a world in itself. Be careful, my good Father Huntly. Be careful! the old priest said to himself as he walked through the house to his study, driven, he realized, by fear and guilt, but also eagerness.

In my first three months there, Father Huntly, we put a new roof on the rectory and had both the church and rectory fumigated as well as painted inside and out. The previous pastor apparently had let things go because of illness. I came to know my parishioners and was amazed by their beauty and generosity, but above all by their unquestioning acceptance of me. There were baptisms, weddings, calls to sick beds, funerals, feast days, sermons to prepare, and the occasional en route missionary to entertain. In short, the usual full schedule of any country priest.

Things finally settled into routine and my eyes became accustomed to surroundings more rugged, apart from those acres set to sugarcane, than I'd expected. There were sections of dense jungle grown up over old lava fields, and other more open areas that first appeared accessible but really were almost impassable because of the loose lava chunks, like furnace clinkers piled deep. The church and rectory sat on an odd, pie-shaped piece of land—the apex behind the church jutted into a thick scrub of guava and other low growth. I thought it might be a good idea to acquire more land on either side and maybe more in back to even out that sharp angle. For starters, our cemetery would soon have to be enlarged. I also envisioned a grotto to Our Lady in a grove of plumeria; a community hall for functions; a small dorm for transient cane workers; possibly even our own school one day. The budget was nowhere near supporting most of this. Yet nothing, no job, now seemed impossible or out of the question. Amazing! I was my father's son after all. Possibilities hung in the air wherever I looked, and I threw myself into parish work. Soon I was exhausted—inevitable, I suppose. When I read at all nights, it wasn't Hopkins or Merton, but Agatha Christie, and my eyes sealed shut after only a page or so. I don't think I even dreamed. Did enough of that during the day.

The land surrounding the church grounds belonged to a man named Tomas Koe, whose wife Elena was a parishioner. I thought we could easily acquire some land from them. Maybe, I thought, they might even be willing to donate it to the church. From there on the rest would be simple. My parishioners were resourceful and willing and could clear the guava scrub and put up a building in no time. Oh, there'd be gardens as well. Vegetables. Flowers. Pathways. I was happy.

But Tomas Koe had other plans. Elena brought her husband to an evening get-together at the rectory, and I managed to speak to him in private. He wasn't a large man; he was of average height, like me, though considerably thinner. Yet he immediately reminded me of my father who was well over six feet, and one of those close-mouthed Wisconsin farmers of enormous dignity who project a kind of humility that said, I know what I can do and can't. Tomas's eyes were a deep, contemplative brown, his skin coppery and smooth. A handsome, reticent man. His black hair showed a bit of gray here and there. Only his teeth weren't good, and he smiled self-consciously. There was something else, too, something I was only half-aware of, distracted as I was by my own self-consciousness. The man was calm but intensely calm, paradoxically, and the air surrounding him seemed to be rippling. Have you ever looked at the surface of a lake, Father Huntly, when a school of fish is right there, an inch, say, below the surface? The water suddenly dimples and swells and undulates, and you know something's there, but you don't know exactly what. Well, that's how the air around Tomas seemed that night. I have since learned there is a Hawaiian word for this quality: li li, which has to do with spirituality. The word is also used to describe heat waves from some beneficent source. But that first night, I was too nervous to fully take in what I was seeing and could only think, What a curious, interesting man. I must ask someone about him. These were background thoughts while I rattled on, doing most of the talking, outlining the problems as I saw them and sketching out my plans. I shamelessly hinted at my hope of a donation. Tomas's thoughtful silence deepened the impression that I was in the presence of my father, whose rootedness, to his land, his opinions, his "way" had always been a barrier between us. I felt a sharp twinge of inferiority and doubt and guilt, as I often had with my father. This man, I sensed, did not fall asleep nights reading Agatha Christie, or its Hawaiian equivalent.

"Mr. Koe," I said finally, "will you at least consider selling us a parcel?"

"I think no."

"You don't even want to consider it? Half an acre, say? What about that scrubby bit? You don't really need that, do you?"

"I cannot sell."

"Ah. Well." Why not? I wondered. "At least think about it," I begged, "and consider my offer open."

I extended my hand and Tomas shook it warmly enough, but the matter seemed closed.

In the next weeks I went to work flattering Elena Koe about her singing, and talking to her about my plans—my hopes, really. "Just think," I'd say, "a nice hall for dinners and parties after baptisms, Elena. Wouldn't that be fine?" She, sweet woman, always agreed but said little. I baptized their son Michael and two years later, their daughter, Juana Lani. By then I'd given up trying to convince Tomas to come to church "just to see what we were up to."

I'd learned that Tomas was the grandson of a Hawaiian priest, or kahuna, and this grandfather came from a long line of temple priests, one of whom served the great Kamehameha when he built the temple— heiau, as it is called—to a Hawaiian war god at Kawaihai, not far from where I'm now living. And it was from this grandfather that Tomas had inherited his tract of land. Originally it'd been far more than ten acres, I heard, and was bestowed upon an ancestor by a high chief of the island. Over time, though, the tract had eroded bit by bit, for various reasons, until Tomas's ten acres were all that remained. Those ten acres formed what had once been the heart of the whole. A sacred place, some told me, much beloved by Madame Pele, the Hawaiian goddess of the volcano. The lava "trees" on the land were believed to be testimony of this. I didn't know what lava trees were but soon found out. Black misshapen columns vaguely tree-like and formed when a lava flow enveloped the living trees, causing them to burn away from the inside. When the lava cooled, first *on the outside, it left a more or less hollow "replica" of a tree. Quite a frightening show of Madame Pele's "endearment."*

I was beginning to understand why people regarded Tomas with great deference and possibly even fear. Intermarriages had diluted his Hawaiian blood somewhat, but not, people apparently believed, his inherited power. They assured me, though, that Tomas's ancestors were not among the deadly hoomanamana, *the lowest orders of* kahunas *who practiced sorcery, but rather the religious kind—the healers, prophets, temple priests, and so on. They tried to convince me that these* kahunas *were my equivalents in the "old way," as rigorously trained in religious law and ritual and devoted to the service of God and man as I myself was. But the implicit message still was: Don't take such a fellow lightly.*

Well. There were a lot of stories, too, though it was hard, if not impossible, to sort out fact from embellishment. When I asked a parishioner about "Mr. Koe," here is something of what I'd get. First, wariness until I assured the person of my high regard for Tomas. Then I might hear, often in great detail, how, for example, Tomas prevented a Mr. Ita, an enraged sugarcane worker, from destroying a boss's house after being fired. Mr. Ita had a wrecking bar and started by smashing out the door and windows, then progressed to the furnishings and walls. Tomas simply walked through the unhinged front door, found an unbroken chair, and sat down. When Mr. Ita finally saw him there, he was so startled and astonished, he dropped the wrecking bar and consented to talk to Tomas, after weeping like some child. Tomas, I was told, saved that house and saved poor Mr. Ita from prison, or worse.

Oh, the stories! Tomas was called upon to calm every imaginable storm, from domestic to civic. Often, his appearance, as with Mr. Ita, was simply enough to work wonders. Sometimes he brought herbs or medicines of his own. The local doctor never seemed to mind being upstaged, figuring, I suppose, that if the patient improved, or at least didn't die, it was quite all right. I heard of Tomas being called to sickbeds and deathbeds; Tomas laying on hands to treat headaches, broken bones, bunions, rheumatism, even tumors! Everywhere, Tomas confronting chaos of one sort or another and imparting order. Just my luck, I thought uncharitably. A witch doctor! Was I jealous? Oh yes. Was I a bit scared? You bet, especially when I happened to remember that first night I'd met him at the rectory, and how the air around him went all swirly.

The whole thing seemed to indicate that the Church obviously hadn't eradicated the roots of the earlier paganism, but had more or less given a new vocabulary and new costumes to the old figures. It started me think-ing about Christianity as a spiritual fertility cult with parallels to other, earlier cults. For my own good, and for the good of my parishioners, I tried to repress such thinking and confessed it as a sin of intellectual pride to my confessor in Hilo. It was depressing that many of my people seemed capable of accepting two religious beliefs at once, seemingly without ever being bothered by guilt or doubt.

This "dualism," if you will, was all the more evident during the vol-canic eruptions of 1968, which inundated the village of Kapoho only a few miles away. People performed many sacrifices to Madame Pele then, throwing offerings into craters—a chicken, a bottle of gin, flowers. I won-dered if I should conduct something along the lines of a parish retreat, or study sessions, but by then my earlier enthusiasm for projects had worn thin. I was usually tired by two in the afternoon and longed for, crazily, a good snowstorm to put everything on hold. The months of glaring sun and heat, my infernal rash, had wrung me out. Nights were better. So were the rare, cool, rainy days when the sky with its low clouds reminded me of home. I did try to fight my lethargy and the guilt one feels when projects are left half-finished or badly done. As an antidote, I used to drive up Mauna Loa just to shiver in the cold thin air. Invigorated after one such drive, I decided to test my courage and have another talk with Tomas.

I hadn't visited Elena and Tomas at home before and half expected a homesteader's cabin sort of thing, but a path through the jungle opened on a clearing with a red cinder drive lined with poinsettia and Royal palms. On either side of this drive were terraced vegetable plots and tree ferns shading beds of anthurium. Beyond the house was a stand of Nor-folk pine. The house itself was modest—the usual tin roof and wood siding painted barn red, and a wide, covered lanai across the front, but its symmetrical lines and its position at the end of the drive suggested the grace and elegance of an eighteenth-century English country house. I felt something of that awe one feels when walking into a grand church. All that effort. All that design. It suggested a kind of sympathetic magic: if this, then maybe, somewhere, on a far greater scale, something truly mag-nificent. Tomas—more likely Tomas's father—had carved all this out of scrub and jungle, no small feat given the nature of things here. This place is truly Eden after the Fall. Tomas's estate, bordered by jungle, seemed a heroic undertaking. If he broke a leg, say, or was sick for a few months, the jungle would roll back in like a tidal wave. The thought gave me shivers, but only in retrospect did I regard it as a foreshadowing. At the time I saw his place as an expression of great faith.

That first day I visited, Tomas welcomed me with gracious reserve. Over the months, I'd formed a romantic image of him on the order of the old Hawaiian kings, loincloth and broad shoulders and feathered capes; yet even in his short-sleeved shirt and loose khaki trousers, Tomas did have regal bearing. Elena served lime drinks as we sat on a sagging couch on the lanai *overlooking the gardens. I started out by praising to the skies his many accomplishments, and he accepted it all with modest poise. A passing shower left the palms and poinsettias and the ti plants around the lanai glittering in low sunlight. The scent of rain rose up off the warm earth and the heated cinder drive, and all at once I felt terribly envious. I was the stranger, the one in exile. What did I have in comparison? And so on. Those crazy questions that flood over you at a time like that hit me hard: Had I made a big mistake with my life? What should I do now? You get the idea.*

Of course a person fights such moments, and in the next minute I was a Roman Catholic priest again, with people to look after and a parish to develop.

"Tomas," I said, trying to put a businessman's firm tone into my words. "I really must do something about that angle of land behind the church. It's no good to the parish as it is, and we really do need more room. I hate like heck to beg, and believe me, I wouldn't bother you if it weren't absolutely necessary. It's not for me personally," I stressed, "but for all the people." Tomas didn't say anything, and for some reason, this time, his silence gave me hope. Lord, I thought, please. *A community hall, I prayed. Gardens— And of course, it* was *for me. It would redeem me, prove my effectiveness. It would cancel that threatening sense of failure. Or at least postpone it.*

Tomas finally spoke. "This land for papaya," he said. "Passion fruit. Maybe citrus, yeah?" He used his right hand like a dancer, shaping these illusory trees.

"Melon," he said, shaping round forms. "Orchid," and he waved his hand like a wand, though only he could see its effect. "Anthurium. Wholesale, eh? Mango. Banana."

Tomas had big plans. He would overextend himself just like farmers in the Midwest and then go under. But that wasn't all. "Shop," he said. "Pahoa shop," and he formed long tables piled high with crushed ice, fruit, and vegetables. "That way," he said, motioning to the right. "That way," to the left. "All, all, all."

His hands, palms upward like a visionary's, made as if to raise growing things toward the sky, but all I could see beyond the neat vegetable beds was impossible jungle. Did he mean to cut down those huge trees and farm every square inch of soil? But of course he didn't. Not the ancient trees. Not Madame Pele's grove. Obviously, Tomas wanted the land kept for his children, for Madame Pele herself, maybe. So, make part of the acreage work to save the whole. And, who knows, maybe even add to it, reclaim something of what had been lost.

Still, I was amazed. "Tomas," I said, "you're one man. Only one."

"One man, yeah!" He laughed and took a homemade cigarette from his shirt pocket, spilling shreds of tobacco over his lap. "One! Then more. Look Michael. Look Juana, eh? You come back fifteen year, eh? That way! That way! That way!"

He raised one slippered foot to the couch and leaned back, smoking with the greatest pleasure. Those long brown arms, all veiny, reminded me of the tough vines encircling the massive trees I'd passed while walking in. Oh, he was happy, imagining his empire. Humility—nothing. He had no idea at all, it seemed, of his limitations, nor of the limitations imposed by life itself, plain old arbitrary circumstances.

To tell you the truth, I was a little afraid for him. My own natural inclination is to brood, to worry, and never, never, never trust—too much—in a moment's happiness. I wanted to warn him.

"Do you think it wise— Do you think you should count on that?"

He brushed the air as if he were stroking an invisible pony. "Michael," he said. "Juana. Then, ta, ta, ta, ta—" He laughed again.

I recognized passion when I saw it. "So. That's that. I understand why you can't part with any of your land." I did, too. At home, farmland passed down from generation to generation is pretty much sacred. You break up acreage only under the greatest duress.

"Well, thank you, Tomas, for your time. Please tell Elena this drink really hit the spot."

Tomas glanced at me with an expression of surprise and pity, as if it had just dawned on him how needy I was. Had I sounded that bad? I blamed it on my old fatigue coming on, and it was getting dark by then. I didn't relish the thought of the long walk back out to the road.

"Look," I said. "I understand. Really. Don't worry about it, OK? Something else might turn up." I stood. Tomas remained seated.

"Maybe I fix that angle for you," he said. "I come to you. You get man, and we fix it up."

Man? Did he mean a lawyer? A surveyor? I sat down again, the air knocked out of me. "The angle?"

"Yeah, yeah! We make it straight, eh? For Elena. Her god." His hand showed what he would do.

Lord. And who was I to refuse, despite Tomas's words relegating Him to some lesser pantheon. God was God. He'd understand. "Great!" I shouted. "Wonderful!" We made arrangements, and then it was time to go. Did I have a light? I thought he meant a match, but he was talking about a flashlight.

"Big crack heah, big crack deah." These he drew and showed what would happen if I strayed off the main path. "People, dey go walk in the jungle and no come back, eh?"

I'd heard stories about that—the deep earth cracks, fissures in the lava actually, caves and lava tubes, everything hidden by vegetation. I'd be careful, you bet.

He loaned me a flashlight and I set off. That's all I needed, I thought, was to fall in some hole. So much for my plans. It had gotten dark fast and I couldn't see much beyond the path. Fear started clanking away inside me, stiffening my movements. I came to the stand of big trees that reminded me of old Tarzan movies. The flashlight's beam skimmed over their huge trunks sheathed in heavy vines with big waxy green leaves. I almost laughed out loud. Tomas was nuts if he thought he could set land like this into neat cucumber and melon beds or whatever. It was the old business, the proverbial reach exceeding the grasp. Maybe he'd come to his senses and there would be more than just the half acre he'd conceded. Be patient, I told myself. Everything might work out.

Caught in these thoughts, I somehow missed a slight veering and wound up on a grassy trail that led deeper into the jungle. Bamboo orchids, white in the moonlight, appeared to be moths fluttering over a lumpy carpet of fern and grasses. This was no third-growth Wisconsin wood but a spooky, primitive place, parts of which probably dated back to the first life on this island. The trail ended abruptly, and my feet sank in sharp lava clinkers that scraped my ankles. Still, something was in control, giving its pathetic commands to do this, do that—barely holding back terror. I turned one way and then another, trying to find the trail. Nothing doing. Soon I began seeing fissures everywhere, inches in front of me. I'd stop suddenly, my heart wild, and then be afraid to move.

Clouds drifted over the moon, and in the darkness a large bird flew low overhead. I could hear the creaking of its wings and feel the whispery displacement of air. I thought of owls back home, those great night predators who could break the back of a cat or small dog in one strike and carry it off. Mosquitoes found me, but at least theirs was a recognizable sound belonging to the daylight world. What I liked less were the damp, earthy breezes I imagined wafting up from the earth cracks all around. I knelt down—sank down, really—willing to trust only those few inches. It didn't help when I heard, or imagined I did, Tomas intoning some long, intricate chant, trade winds and jungle whipping the drum-beat syllables around so that they seemed to be coming from several directions. I knelt there shivering and tried to pray, but a sensation, a sickness of some kind, overwhelmed me, and at that moment I felt that not even prayer would help. If I'd been one of those knights in the Grail stories, I would have been washed up then and there for such a huge failure of heart.

Irrational, you say?—to feel like that when terror simply has the upper hand? Simply? Faith is never rational; it's the heart responding. And what better time for it to click in and do its work than against all that? But to be empty of everything except the terror—

The priest paused to reach for his cigar box holding the sermon notes and filled out an index card under the heading, Faith and the Garden of Gethsemene. Then without further thought, he was back, scribbling fast.

. . . Tomas's flashlight, growing dim, sent its frail tunnel of light into the grasses, while I knelt there weeping as you do when you dream your own death—the tears just coming, and almost sweet. Eventually I must have dozed off, huddled on those few damp inches. At first light I awoke and saw that I'd wandered onto a secondary path. If there were earth cracks nearby, I certainly wasn't in imminent danger of falling into one. Everything sparkled with drops of moisture, an enamel green everywhere.

The pink bamboo orchids on their tall, frail stems. The incense smell of wet fern. Oh, lovely! All lovely. But as after a bad night's sleep filled with nightmares something—some residual despair—remained, and I felt wounded in my very soul.

How could I go on, giving sermons, hearing confessions, saying the Mass? I should just go back to the mainland. Go somewhere and start over. Then I got panicky, thinking, do what? Sell insurance? Teach? Even there you needed certification that would take time to acquire. I suddenly regarded my parishioners in a new light—people who were carpenters and fishermen and cane workers and schoolteachers. They all had valuable skills. They married and raised children and taught them important things! Oh, Tomas, I thought, stomping down hard as I walked and causing flickers of pain to shoot upward from those swollen ankles. Did you do this? Did you reduce me to this? How come you didn't see me out to the road? It would have been the courteous thing to do. But no. Did you want me getting lost and scared? Are you mocking me with your witch doctor tricks? Are you trying to prove something? All right, I thought. So be it. Then I no longer felt hollow, but filled with purpose and conviction and—oh, awful!—the bile of anger. I was so mad I threw the flashlight with all my might into the jungle and heard it crash through leaves and thud down somewhere—breaking, I hoped—

The old priest looked up from his words, surprised to see the ocean forming out of the thinner gray of dawn. He refilled his pen and carefully wiped the gold nib clean, then let his writing hand drop to his side. In his thoughts he addressed the younger priest. I was running on empty, Father Huntly. Can you understand?

THREE

"Yes, Kani!" he called. "I'm up. Come in!"

Kani entered his study with a tray. She was a strongly-built middle-aged woman wearing her waitress outfit for the Mauna Kea resort, a long muumuu with white eyelet trim at the high collar and puffy short sleeves. Its leafy print was cobalt blue on white, and she'd pinned two white plumeria blossoms in her hair.

"So you working, eh?"

"Oh, not working, not like you!" He pushed aside papers, making room for the wood tray that held a cup of fresh-ground Kona coffee, orange juice, a bowl of cornflakes, and half a papaya with a wedge of lemon.

"You eat now, yeah, Father? They pay twenty dollar for this at the hotel."

"I know. Thank you, but you really shouldn't bother, Kani, when you have so much to do in the morning." Kani had a family to see to, then had to get ready herself and drive ten miles or so to the resort, stopping at his place on the way. On Friday afternoons, she cleaned his house, claiming he didn't do it right himself, and smashed whatever water bugs were so foolish as to appear while she was there. Twice a week, at least, she brought him an evening meal, often excellent leftovers from the hotel and sometimes a big jar of *saimin*, the noodle soup he loved. He could make several meals of the saimin alone. On Saturday afternoons she sold her flower leis at the Kona-Kailua airport, where she wore a red and white muumuu and wide-brimmed straw hat trimmed with feathers. Two of her children attended the University of Hawaii at Hilo, partly as the result of all her work. He was glad she had taken him under her wing but felt unworthy. He suspected Juana Koe's hand in the matter.

"If I not come," she said now, "you don't eat."

"I eat. Really."

"You eat scraps, yeah? You an' Buffy." Buffy was the name she'd given to the half-wild gray and white cat who'd recently taken up residence at the priest's house. Kani's voice was stern, her usual way of making a joke. He smiled, but he knew the reason she stopped by each morning. Should he die in the night, she did not want him to have to lie there alone for who knew how long.

"Bye-bye, now. See you maybe later." From the kitchen, she called, "Buf-fy! *Buf-*fy!" wanting to give the treacherous cat, who often lashed out at the priest's ankles for no conceivable reason, a saucer of milk, just as she put down saucers of cream for the skinny cats appearing in the morning at the Mauna Kea's posh terrace restaurant, to the amusement of its well-to-do patrons.

"Buf-fy! *Whooo-oo!* Come."

He heard her car backing down the drive and felt a pang of loneliness, self-pity, and guilt at his old-man's immobility and comparative uselessness. But the coffee revived his spirits, and there was his work, waiting. He couldn't believe he wasn't the least bit sleepy, after being up nearly all night.

Something bumped down. The cat?—Jumping? After a water bug?

"Tomas?"

His heart veered back and forth a while, then settled, and the house, too, was quiet. He picked up his pen and continued.

. . . *Within a month, Father Huntly, the parish owned an extra half acre, and a crew began clearing work. Nervously at first, I should say, because to them it was still Tomas's land. Plans for a new addition to the cemetery grounds lay on the dining room table. The hall would have to wait a bit.*

In time Elena sent her daughter Juana, but not Michael, for religious instruction. Juana was a beautiful child and extremely bright. I wondered about Michael, and one day had a chance to question Elena. She was polite but evasive. "That child was baptized a Christian, Elena," I said. "This is no good, you know. This will cause all kinds of hoohoo," *meaning troubles. She was taking deep breaths. Her eyelids trembled as she half-closed her eyes, hearing me out. I sensed I was taking out on her my irrational anger against Tomas, but I couldn't stop. When I did finish, finally, she asked in a frightened, nearly inaudible voice if I could "undo" the baptism. Poor Elena. I'm afraid I read her the riot act that day. She had to talk to Tomas, had to convince him, I said. The boy was a* Christian. *Words to that effect. If I let this matter slide, I was thinking, it'll be a sign, a precedent. I had to be strict, and I had to win.*

I did. Not too long afterward, Michael came for instruction, but Elena gave me the cold shoulder whenever we chanced to meet, and she stopped singing in the choir. I was surprised she came to church at all.

A few years later I learned from Michael's teacher at the elementary school in the village that he had great hopes for the boy. I casually mentioned Tomas's plans, and the man reacted strongly. "We need doctors!" he said. "Good government people for this island! Our children must develop their full potential!"

"Then you must talk to Tomas," I said. "Tell him these things."

His sudden retreat into silence told me that no matter how strongly he felt about it, he didn't wish to meddle in a kahuna's *affairs.*

"All right," I said. "I'll speak to him, then." Sheer bravado. I was scared, too, deep down, but wouldn't dream of letting it show.

In the next months the teacher became my unwitting accomplice. Scholarship funds were already in the works, and when things were finally organized, both Michael and Juana were the first selected to attend an excellent preparatory school in Honolulu, on the island of Oahu, some two hundred and fifty miles away. Michael was to go that fall, Juana, the following year.

I urged the teacher to write a laudatory article for the Hilo newspaper, and it was published, along with the children's photos, to much excitement here in Pahoa. Mrs. Hakutani, the grocer, and Roberto, the baker, displayed the article prominently in their shops. Everyone congratulated Tomas and Elena, and the whole town was honored. Now, Tomas, I thought. Now is the time to say no, forcefully and publicly, if you want to stop the thing. I expected him to. I expected the clippings to come down from the store windows, at his urging. But they didn't, and I guessed the reason why. Tomas was a proud man, as I'd known right from the beginning. And now, I understood, it was a question of not losing face.

"What a wonderful thing!" I'd say whenever I saw Elena or Tomas in the village. "You must be so proud of them!" Oh, I laid it on thick.

"Too far," Tomas told me once. "Across the water, too much, eh?"

"But Tomas, he'll be back, summers and holidays." I'd nearly said Christmas! "And he'll learn so much better there. It's a grand opportunity!"

He liked nothing about it, I sensed, except that his children had achieved some important distinction, and by extension so had he.

"You really don't want to limit their choices, do you, Tomas?"

He looked alarmed then, and worried. I went on, pretending to neutrality, rationality, wisdom even. "You know, I think they have to be as free to choose as you yourself are, Tomas. Otherwise, things will never pan out. They'll be unhappy and so will you. That's how it goes, believe me."

"I will think some more," he said.

"Yes, do. It's for the good of your farm, you know. Ultimately, I mean."

Ah, that *hit home! It gave me an idea, too. I wrote the principal of the school in Honolulu, asking him to write to Tomas personally, listing all the excellent tropical agriculture courses Michael would be able to take if he went on to the university afterward. The man did, sending me a note to this effect, and when I was certain Tomas must have received the letter, I worked this angle, never mentioning, of course, that I knew about his letter from Honolulu. I'd begin by asking him about his crops, and he'd respond with enthusiasm, telling me of some new development, a new vegetable that was doing better than expected; the vanda orchid project, which was becoming a success. Oh, I envied him this, I must admit. Envied his spirit and energy and the fact that he was getting things done, whereas I always seemed to be spinning my wheels, running from one nuisance task to another, with nothing getting* properly *done.*

Have you ever faced this sort of thing, Father Huntly? A leaky roof, say, that's never quite fixed no matter how many times somebody climbs up there to fuss with it. Or, the termite fumigation people from Hilo rescheduling again and again, all stupid details! Where was the intensity and depth? Everything gone. Where was the spirituality? I'd think, staring into the grimy cluttered space that was the village garage. Banging away at the carburetor with a wrench, I'd tell myself to make that a holy act. What a joke. I was fragmented all to pieces, always thinking of what had to be done in the next minute, the next hour, the next day, and losing the present altogether. Thomas Merton found a kind of holy peace while walking the woods around his monastery and marking trees to be cut. He also worked with the loggers and found joy and spirituality in that. Well, the explanation's simple. He was a saint.

But I see I've gone off the track again. The business of the letter wasn't the end of my machinations, Father Huntly. I set in motion another

powerful offensive. Shortly after Michael's graduation from the elemen-
tary school, I organized a luau *on the church grounds to celebrate the*
achievement. Nearly the whole village came to honor the Koe family and,
above all, Tomas himself. He took it all with his usual poise and reti-
cence, but before the evening was through, he spoke to me in private, at
first quite cordially, thanking me for the festivity, but then said some-
thing that caused a chill to zoom through me. "It is good of you, a
malihini, *to do this for us." Malihini. The word means* newcomer, foreigner, *but also has the darker connotation of stranger. And the way he*
looked at me then, with those intently calm eyes of his. I thought, He
knows! He knows what I've been up to!

"Oh, Tomas," I said, "I do wish you the best, and the best for your
children, too. Please believe me."

Later I kept thinking how he'd stressed that word, malihini, *so deli-*
cately. It was the closest Tomas had ever come, in my hearing, to
expressing an insult, to showing anger, distrust.

After that, I prepared myself for bad news, and when the teacher finally
called me that summer to say Tomas had finally agreed to let Michael
"try it," I was stunned for a moment, then oddly frightened. It struck me,
for the first time, just how badly the thing could backfire. I was thinking,
then, in terms of obvious disasters. Michael hit by a car, Michael lost in
the city and coming to some harm, Michael terribly homesick and doing
poorly, uprooted. For days I went around shaken and absent-minded.

My confessor in Hilo—elderly, kind, but on the brink of senility, I
feared—said I should go back to the mainland on a retreat. Sort every-
thing out there. A change was in order.

"The Islands aren't for everyone," he said. We were in his sitting room
that looked out on the lights of Hilo below us. In the winter months it
rains quite a bit in Hilo, and the room felt damp and musty. There were
patches of mildew up in the corners. It was raining heavily that night,
and rain sluicing off the wide eaves fell on huge plants clustered under
the screened windows. I thought of Tomas's jungle. Father Sturman had
some sort of insect repellent burning in a little dish—a foul, irritating
scent, and for the longest time he'd been kneeling before a blackened fire-
place, trying to get a fire going. He had no dry kindling, apparently, and
kept balling up newspaper and sticking it under two charred logs that
hadn't been split. Our conversation up to this point was desultory, broken
by Father Sturman's exclamations of "Well! Now we have it!" Or, "Any

minute now—" His supply of newspaper was low, and pretty soon, I thought, he'd give up and we'd just make do with the damp.

"That's OK," I'd say every so often. "Please don't bother. It's really warm enough." Anxious, you know, to talk about myself.

"Oh no!" he'd cry. "It's almost going now. Watch!" And whompf, newspaper caught and flames swept over the logs, only to die back, leaving the logs quite intact.

My visits with Father Sturman were often like this. He bending over backwards to make it an occasion, a party. On a coffee table stood a bottle of Jameson's Irish whiskey and two ordinary water glasses. The bottle was half gone, and I wondered about that. Next to the whiskey was a bowl of damp pretzels. All that had been brought out with great ceremony. The room was getting murky with smoke despite the moist gusts of wind blowing in. I watched tropical fish swimming about in a big tank placed in a wall niche that Father Sturman had said was especially designed by the house builders to contain Buddhist figures. The fish were supposed to make one restful and serene, he'd said, but it didn't work for me. It was getting late and I had a twenty-mile drive back in all that rain.

"Father—"

"Please. Call me Mark."

"OK. The thing is, I—" Worried, of course, about the next day.

"There! Now it's drawing properly! That was the trouble all along. Ah!" He rubbed his smudged hands before the tenuous flames and then could hardly get himself upright. A small man, nearly as wide as he was tall, or short, rather. He looked all mussy and disheveled, and his gray hair badly needed a wash. His eyeglasses, too, could use a good cleaning. An old man, I thought, in a dank room smelling of old man. Would I be like that one day, I worried—desperately hanging on to "company" in order to dispel whatever terrible loneliness? "Oof!" he cried. "Rheumatism! You know we grow webbed feet here!"

"Really?" He told me this every time I visited.

"That's for sure!" He took out a gray-looking handkerchief and blew his nose hard. "Sinuses. Allergies. You name it. We may have been creatures of the deep once, according to the evolutionists, but we certainly can't handle the wet now, and of course that makes one wonder—"

"Oh, I don't think—"

"You're lucky, though, in Pahoa. More sun there. Here we walk around in a rain cloud for three months."

"That's true, yes."

He filled each glass with the Jameson's. No ice, no water, no nothing. This he called Irish wine.

"I have to drive back," I said, refusing the drink.

"Stay here! We'll have a good talk and you can get back first thing early in the morning." This suggestion brought him to the edge of the couch. His voice was all excitement and urgency. But the thought of sleeping under musty sheets, with that insect stuff burning on a night table depressed me. Also the fact that I'd always refused before and would again have to deal with his childlike disappointment. I found myself accepting the whiskey.

"Ah! Wonderful!" He swallowed what I thought was a dangerous amount all at once and launched into a monologue about the seasons, as one from the Midwest understood the word. This led to extended reminiscing about his earlier days in northern Michigan, where he'd coached high school basketball (I couldn't imagine it), taking a number of Class-B championships. He went on in great detail about the cold winters and furnaces going out and pipes freezing. By then the Jameson's had begun to taste pretty good, but the smoke from the smoldering logs was making my eyes very tired. I lapsed into my own nostalgia, thinking of the farm and of my brothers and their families all settled close by, still connected. I must have looked pretty gloomy. The room seemed awfully quiet then, except for the rain, and I became aware of Father Sturman staring at me, sizing me up, as it were.

"Now," he said. "Tell me."

You know, when you're having a bad time and somebody says that, you pretty much fall apart. There's gratitude for the human closeness, which more or less tears you apart, but at the same time it suddenly all seems hopeless and impossible, even to say anything, get it said. And I was dizzy, too, a little drunk and afraid of becoming maudlin or whatever. A rush of self-pity tightened my throat—felt like a fist there. Oh, I wanted to bawl my head off. Then I felt terrible for Father, doing his best in this far-away place, in this musty damp that was wrecking him. Also, it was late. I knew he must be tired, on top of everything, and what I had to say would take a long time. Hours. Maybe all week. "Tomorrow—" I managed. "When we're more—"

"It's already tomorrow!" That joke deserved more Jameson's, he seemed to think, and emptied the rest into my glass.

"No, please, I couldn't—"

"So. You were saying?"

I hadn't been saying anything but thought, well here goes, and started out—by way of introduction, I was thinking—with Thomas Merton and how he fought certain doubts—not about his faith per se, but about directions in his life. Choices. God's will for him, and so on. I went on and on, getting all wound up in my fine-tuned intellectual analysis of this and that, always always always skirting the real problem. Shame filled me as if I really were making a confession when I described the relationship between Tomas and myself. "It's impossible to really convert these people!" I cried at one point. "This whole business is impossible. We don't belong here. I don't. I—" then came the words I'd dreaded above all others. "I don't know what I believe anymore. If I—Oh, Lord—"

After a long while, it seemed, Father Sturman spoke. Mildly. "Waken morning by morning," he said. I thought he might be drunk, too, and trying to tell me what time to get up the next day.

"I'm sorry?"

"Isaiah. He wakeneth morning by morning," said Father Sturman, quoting, oddly, from the King James Version.

"Oh! Right." I waited for more. Now that everything was out of the bag pretty much, I wanted to hear what he would say. I wanted to be comforted. Coddled, maybe, and assured. I wanted to talk about faith, the nature of, the difficulties of, and so on. I wanted to hear that he'd had a similar experience and had gotten through it. But he sat there gazing at his half-burnt logs and wouldn't say anything. Maybe he was of the old school, distrusting "discussions," analyses, probing, riding a thing into the ground and nothing coming of it. Maybe he thought it was enough that I had broken down finally and talked. Now, clearly, he wanted me to meditate on Isaiah's words, strange as anything in Zen, to my mind. Then, after another lengthy silence, he said what froze my heart: Go back. To the mainland. Make a good retreat. Do some reading and praying. All the greatest saints, he said, have gone through dark nights of the soul. I was no saint, though, and I felt doomed. Then, to cheer me up—and *end our "talk"—he told that old joke about the monk who gets to speak once every ten years. I'm sure you've heard it. After his first decade in the monastery, he says he's not too happy about the food. After twenty years, he has a few bad things to say about his bed and the lack of heat. Finally, after his third decade, he says he doesn't care for the monastery at all and wants to go home. No wonder, the brothers tell him. You've done nothing but complain for thirty years. Father Sturman took off his cloudy glasses at this point and laughed, mostly by himself. He put on his glasses again and said, "Don't worry, it'll all straighten itself out. You'll see." I shouldn't feel too bad, he said, but I couldn't help it. I'd spent so much of my life reading and praying and thinking—and what?*

The next morning he held onto the car door as I was sitting in the driver's seat, ready to leave, and said, "When He closes a door, He opens a window." I couldn't believe it—that simple little saying we tell grade school kids, and there he was, looking all profound. At that moment I sensed in my bones his perfect faith, way too great for—

What? the old priest asked himself at his desk. Way too great for what? The answer came. *Words.* Father Sturman was a saint, maybe, whereas look at *him.* Fiddling with words. Still. After all this time. He rubbed his cramped fingers, then had his papaya drizzled with lemon juice. The cornflakes would be for supper if Kani didn't stop by on her way home. Resting, he looked out at the plane of ocean, blue and hazy. Why hadn't he taken Father Sturman's advice and gone back? The answer didn't take much thinking. Pride. He could admit failure to himself, but not to his family, his relatives—all waiting, he'd sensed, for exactly that.

Like them or not, the priest thought, words were coming, coursing down from somewhere. He refilled his pen.

. . . I didn't go back for a retreat, Father Huntly. For a time I just muddled along, hoping for the best. Things were quiet in Pahoa, though not in the world at large. It was the time of the Vatican Reforms, all those huge changes intended to bring about some great new renaissance of faith among the world's Catholics. I'm ashamed to say it worked just the opposite for me. I deeply missed the old Latin hymns, the old "Tantum Ergo" and "O Salutaris" and all the rest, and I often got all mixed up in the new liturgy—to everyone's amusement. Sometimes, in the middle of saying Mass, I'd lose concentration and begin spouting Latin. Dominus

vobiscum! *I'd sing, and the people, after hesitating a bit, would respond in the old way.* Et cum spiritu tuo! *The Lord be with you. And with your spirit! I'd catch myself after a bit and swing back into English, and so would my congregation. Oh, the stumbling and bumbling! We were like foreigners trying so very hard to speak fluently in a new language. You probably are wondering at this, having grown up with the English liturgy, but for me, well, I'd taken Latin to heart, you see. It was all bound up with my being a priest, and to lose that on top of all the rest, as I saw it— Well. Not an easy time.*

On weekdays, if no one came to the early morning Mass—rare—I'd celebrate it in Latin, the old words making me so happy, telling me connections hadn't been severed after all. Per omnia saecula saeculorum! *I'd sing.* World without end! Sed libra nos a malo! *But deliver us from evil— Oh, even going so far as to read the Last Gospel, which most strangely, had been removed from the Ordinary of the Mass by the new reforms. How the Latin swelled like grand waves. Listen!* In principio erat Verbum et Verbum erat apud Deum, et Deus erat Verbum! *In the beginning was the Word, and the Word was with God; and the Word was God—*

The old priest had to stop and wipe his eyes. Blow his nose. The Word!—Heart of all things, essence, Mystery.

. . . Oh, Father Huntly, what complicated emotions. There I was in an empty church, certain I wasn't worthy to be saying those words and knowing I shouldn't be saying them, and yet allowing them to fill me with such reverberating sweetness. I was hollow, true—empty, doubtful, scared—but doubt, you see, isn't a positive thing, a thing of substance. Maybe it's just that: a hollowness, a poised waiting, a hunger, a vessel needing to be filled. Those old Latin words gave me courage to keep going, keep thinking that maybe I wasn't all washed up as a priest but still on the way to becoming a good one. Just go through the motions, I kept telling myself. Don't lose hope.

When I see my friend Kani in her long muumuu, I'm reminded of those days, oddly. Such an outfit is now regarded as traditional Hawaiian attire. Tourists have come to expect it. There are pictures and prints in the museums—artists depicting Hawaiian women. But if you recall, this style of dress evolved from the outfits designed by the good missionaries, our spiritual ancestors. So the tradition reaches back only a short time in the scheme of things. But I can guess what you're thinking. Latin itself wasn't adopted as the language of the liturgy—the Tridentine Mass—until as late as the sixteenth century, and therefore—

The priest sighed, pushing the sheet away from him and recapping his pen. Therefore, what? Somehow he'd strayed into dialectics, or something. An old man's rambling. Father Huntly would toss it away, disgusted. Afternoon sunlight struck the white dishes on the tray—a fury of light—and he had to shut his eyes. Don't mourn change, he told himself. Everything changes. Life is change. Even the Islands, right at that moment, were sinking infinitesimally back into the deep. Don't mourn your lost Latin like a spoiled child. Never mourn change! In change lies hope.

When light no longer jumped from object to object, flashing like heat lightning, he got up stiffly and went into the kitchen to take his pills. The time amazed him. Three in the afternoon and there he was, still in his pajamas and robe.

For the rest of the day he dozed in a chaise lounge, in thin shade thrown by an old *kiawe* tree. The cat, stretched out in the attitude of a high diver, sprawled in deeper shade along the side of the house. The priest's nap consisted of shallow dreaming, bits and fragments, a flickering business more tiring than restful. Once he heard the murmuring voices of many people somewhere in the house. They were looking for him, it seemed, and would at any moment burst out onto the patio and find him. Then the voices slipped away on some inner current and the dream snippets became the usual jumble.

He awoke to a breeze that held a hint of welcome moisture. If not for his achy joints, he would have liked to live higher up on the Kohala slopes, an area people said reminded them of the Scottish Highlands, while he always thought, *Wisconsin.* But his tan hillside stubbled with prickly pear and softened by *kiawe* groves was very nice, too. The Holy Land, he felt, must have been something like this. In his imaginings there were no concrete high rises or highways or bombed cities, but just arid ancient slopes, lavender in the evening, and falling into a luminous sea.

A car was coming up the drive. He sat up too fast, causing the patio to spin and then go dark. Anxiously he waited for things to clear. He had to hide that untouched bowl of cornflakes.

FOUR

He slept well for the first time in weeks and awoke refreshed, eager to continue the writing, but Kani, bawling him out about the corn-flakes, fixed him eggs with toast and stayed until he finished.

"If I'm late, I'm late. Too bad, yeah? You eat!"

He did, but preoccupied with the words, still coming, so many and yet not the heart of it. That still ahead. The worst part. His resolve faltered a bit, but then he looked at Kani, brilliant in blue and white and watching him so fiercely. There was resolve! Courage. Her husband gone and she still brimming with life, ferocity even.

He asked for more toast.

"Good!" She jumped up. "You get strong, yeah?"

"Fat, you mean."

"That's OK, too."

Maybe so. Most of the Hawaiian royals had been huge. It was believed to be a sign of favor, aristocracy, of life itself. And clearly, Kani wasn't having anything to do with fasting hermits.

"I the boss," she said, spreading the toast thick with guava jam. "You eat."

He waved as she backed down the drive, then he hurried to his study, avoiding the cat, who seemed in the mood, that day, for ambushes, skirmishes.

. . . I'm still surprised, Father Huntly, that my confessor, Father Sturman, didn't write to our bishop, suggesting a transfer for me. Maybe he forgot, or maybe he had his reasons. At any rate, it seemed I'd been pretty much forgotten. Maybe they'd remember, I thought, only when I died. I didn't go back on my own, but decided to stick it out, come what may.

Nor did Tomas's children ever return. Oh, they came back for vacations and visits, but they didn't come back body and soul. That's the only way I know how to put it. Pahoa was no longer their home, just as Wisconsin wasn't mine. Juana studied art history at the university in Honolulu and became a curator in a Honolulu museum. She often traveled to Asia for the museum. Michael was a bit more unsettled. He did come back once or twice to help Tomas work his land, but he'd always leave again, shortly. In my day people would say he just needed to see a few things before settling down, sow some wild oats. Juana phrased it differently. Michael, she said, wanted to get his head together. Tomas was putting too much pressure on him. I knew all about that firsthand—those demands and disappointments needing only the language of silences.

Then Elena Koe died after a surprisingly short illness. Pneumonia with complications. I could sense that Tomas held this, everything, against me. He wouldn't come to church for the funeral but did walk with the coffin to the cemetery—on what had been his land. He didn't stay to see dirt cover her coffin. After that, he started letting things go on his place, I heard, and began coming into the village to just sit on a bench outside Roberto's Bakery. Whenever the baker took a break, the two of them would sit there, smoking cigarettes and watching whatever was happening along the road. The baker didn't seem the least bit in awe of Tomas, or nervous around him. I'd see them laughing together like school chums and would wonder what they found to laugh about. When Roberto went back in to work, Tomas would sit there alone. The change in him shocked me. He'd become a small old man who seemed to have nothing better to do than sit on a shady bench, one foot in its green slipper up, the other just touching the narrow sidewalk. I'd say hello when I went for a loaf of Roberto's sweet-bread, but Tomas wasn't having any of it. He'd pretend not to recognize me, or that he hadn't heard me, or else he'd stare coldly at me until I lost courage and went into the shop.

Should he tell him? the priest wondered. Or would Father Huntly think him loony for sure, and then question all the rest? The thing was too bizarre, uncertain, too strange. He himself couldn't understand it on any rational level. A chill passed over him as he looked up, preparing to see it again: Tomas standing in the hall, on the night of Elena Koe's death, though the priest hadn't known she was dying, nor even ill, but Tomas had come to the rectory and then stood mute in the doorway as if too emotionally overcome to speak. The air around him had puckered and swirled. "Just a moment, Tomas," he'd said. "I'll be right with you." He'd needed to get his kit, and when he turned back to Tomas, the man was gone, though the air still felt unsettled. The hall door was closed. No one was on the *lanai,* nor in the yard. The next morning Mrs. Hakutani called to tell him of Elena Koe's death.

What distressed the old priest most was that even if the event hadn't been a "real" summons to the deathbed, it had been a summons nonetheless, and the priest hadn't obeyed it. In the following weeks, he'd "seen" Tomas in odd places, at odd times. Near the lettuce bed behind the rectory just before sunset, or sometimes appearing to walk up the steps into the church.

And then Tomas had become old and ordinary, the air quiet around him. No, he couldn't tell Father Huntly all that. Maybe it had been, simply, an effect of his own exhaustion. His imagination running wild.

What a time of confusion, Father Huntly! Weren't they better off? I'd argue with myself. Juana, for sure. Unshackled from the past was the way I put it. Free. And who's to say, I'd tell myself, that they wouldn't have chosen similar paths on their own. Also, I couldn't possibly be the only person responsible, what about their teachers? And so on. But then I'd see Tomas alone on that bench and wonder how to loosen and pick apart that knot we call guilt.

To make matters worse—even nightmarish—Tomas's land was threatened in some complicated business involving tax liens. The way he was letting everything go, I thought his mind might have been affected by all his losses. And Juana, who'd just sunk a lot of money into a condominium, wasn't going to be able to help all that much, as far as taxes went.

One evening, quite late, the phone rang at the rectory. A sick call, I thought.

"Father?"

"Yes? Who's this, please?"

A long pause, the hum of long-distance, and then, "Mike. Michael Koe?" As if I wouldn't remember him.

"Michael! Where are you? Are you here?"

"No. With Juana. In Honolulu."

"Oh! Well, good." Of course he must know about his mother, I was thinking, glad to be spared that. And he would have heard of Tomas's troubles, as well. Go easy, I told myself. Don't push.

"I know it's real late, sorry. I just got in."

I wanted to ask from where but held back.

"Father, I've saved up some money and want to go back to school. Graduate school."

"Yes? Where? At the university?" Did they even have graduate programs there? I didn't know but hoped so. I was sure he could hear the waver of falsity in my voice, the pretense of neutral interest.

"On the mainland."

"Oh."

"Stanford."

"I see. What area?" No hiding dread now. Michael picked up on it at once and rattled off something as if afraid I might try and stop him. I caught a word here and there and thought, Oh, medicine. Maybe it'll turn out OK. But then he was saying something about artificial intelligence, and I realized I was way off base and had no idea what he wanted to study, except that whatever it was, it wouldn't help Tomas.

"Father, can you go out and see him for me? Tell him I'm back and— you know, prepare the way, like?"

"I don't understand."

"I can't talk to him, yeah? He looks right through me when he doesn't want to hear something. And now that, now that—my mother—"

"Michael, listen to me. You have to come here on your own. Just come and see him."

"I can't."

Tension poured through the receiver. And I, the guilty party, stood there reaping my reward.

"I feel so rotten, man. Juana, she says go, go. Only I know what's going to happen, yeah? He's so angry at me. He thinks I failed him, that I'm no good—"

"That's not true. Michael? He doesn't—"

"OK. All right. But he wants—he wants too much! You've got to talk to him, Father. Tell him—I mean, explain—" A choked-off, muffled sound, then. Was he crying? Had he been drinking?

"I didn't even know she was sick! How could I know she'd just . . ."

"You couldn't have known. Don't blame yourself, Michael. Surely you musn't! Now, listen. Come back and see your father. Talk to him. What could I possibly say that you can't say yourself, only better?"

More tension. Mute begging. The faint charged hum linking us all. Then, "To forgive me. Let me go."

The next morning I chose my time carefully. Roberto had just gone back into the bakery and Tomas was alone on the bench. Instead of greeting Tomas as I usually did, I sat down alongside him and began to speak. But suddenly needle-prick pains were zooming up my arms, a sensation not unlike frostbitten toes or fingers thawing out. Dizziness came, blurred colors, and I lost control of my speech and sounded like a drunk. I must have slumped against Tomas and felt him recoil. The next think I knew, a cane truck in low gear was passing right in front of me, an awful, angry sound, like something being ripped apart. Tomas was gone.

A few weeks later, in Honolulu, where I went for tests, I learned my carotid arteries were calcifying like coral into fine branches of stone. There were explanations having to do with chemical reactions and blood pressure, but I knew better; the death of the body can only follow where the heart has failed. After the hospital business, I went to see Juana at her museum. We sat in a small courtyard with a splashing fountain and a brilliant magenta bougainvillea against a stone wall.

"Is there any chance you could return to the Big Island, Juana?" I asked. "Not just for a visit, I mean."

Her heavy dark hair was pulled back into a thick braid, and she was wearing a dress of some fine woven fabric. The effect, in that elegant stone courtyard with its turquoise fountain and cloud of flowers, was truly lovely. She might have been a princess in some exquisite illustration or miniature such as those she collected. I couldn't imagine her weeding vegetables with those hands, or spraying papaya, or sorting and bundling carrots in a Pahoa shop. But I had to try.

While she stared at those hands as if distressed by what her father would consider their useless beauty, I told her how I'd tried to speak to Tomas and had gotten nowhere. "He's not himself," I said. "He shouldn't be alone. He wants his vegetable shop. Roberto says that's all he talks about. Even Roberto is worried."

"Oh, Father," she said, "I love him, but what should I do? Should I give up everything here? My life, now, is here."

That now was an accusation whether she meant it to be or not. It was my turn to look down.

"I could go back every weekend," she said, then went into a set speech that sounded rehearsed. Circumstances, chance—whatever—had favored her with gifts that couldn't be denied without causing all kinds of trouble. And because these had been given to her, she must offer them back to the world, or else they would "die" within her. Words to that effect. This couldn't be done in the village, nor even in Hilo. How our pasts, Father Huntly, never quite finish with us! Do you sense this? What a cruel trick that we wind up "giving back" not to those who give to us, but to the anonymous world, to strangers. And yet—Do you know the Maori custom of gift-giving? A great circle of gift-giving, so that one is always giving to a stranger and then receiving from the world in the persona of another stranger.

I could see how Juana was affected by all this. Her wonderful face with Tomas's determination there, the bronze handsomeness, seemed frozen in awareness. She was Juana grappling with her predicament, but at the same time she was the mythic Eve, moments after the Fall, a child aware of her separateness, of the separation.

"My heart is so divided," she said.

We sat there then, watching a small bird alight on the rim of the fountain, blithely accepting its gift. Finally Juana surprised me with a proposal of her own. She wondered if I couldn't get Tomas to come to Honolulu, to her place. Michael would be there. It would be a reunion. Neutral territory, she thought, might dissolve their estrangement. Or at least help. Some place not all bound up with the past.

Good for whom? I wondered. "Juana," I said, "your father won't even say hello to me these days. I don't see how he'd ever agree to come to Honolulu with me. Why don't you and Michael just go and visit him? Surprise him that way? Stay a week or so. Longer."

"Michael's afraid to go home. He feels trapped there. They'll argue and Michael will just take off again."

"You're both afraid of him, it seems. He is a kahuna, isn't he?"

Juana smiled, and I sensed deep down that whatever power Tomas had, he would never use it against his children no matter what. My heart started its jumpy racing. What protection had I, though? I saw Tomas and Roberto sitting on the bench, laughing together. Could it be that my own illness was the result of some curse? Good Lord. It couldn't be, could

it? And Juana was saying, "My father is a good kahuna.*" Ah, I thought,
chilled, but a* kahuna *all the same.*

*She elaborated on her plan. If Tomas and I could just appear one eve-
ning, a surprise visit as far as Michael would know, the shock of it might
be good for both of them. I didn't say what it might do to me. But the
plan was drastic enough and simple enough to perhaps work.*

*"Tomas has never been on a plane before, has he? Nor to Honolulu.
It's going to be awfully traumatic for him."*

*She thought so, too, but believed it was a risk worth taking. "He'll see
that this world does exist, that we're not completely lost here. We haven't
fallen off the face of the earth. He'll see, maybe, there is substance here."
She patted the stone bench. "And value."*

*But that isn't what he wants, I thought. "I don't know, Juana. It's a
tall order."*

"Try," she said. "Please, Father?"

Father. Lord.

The priest and the cat had a late supper of curried chicken and rice
from the Mauna Kea, each dining at opposite ends of the kitchen,
each from an aluminum pie tin; then he washed up, wanting Kani to
find the clean tins in the drying rack the next morning. He wondered
if he'd taken his pills. He couldn't remember. Once the pill container
had slipped from his fingers, and the pills had bounced and rolled
everywhere. He was still finding them. He wondered if Father Huntly
had to take pills of any kind. Probably not.

He saw himself in the Toyota, driving to Pahoa, surprising Father
Huntly. Wouldn't such a visit have more power than a rambling letter? And weren't letters cowardly, really? He could still drive. He still
had his car. He wouldn't be able to navigate the tricky coast highway
zig-zagging along the deep gorges between Honokaa and Hilo—not in
his shaky condition, but there was the Saddle Road between Mauna
Kea and Mauna Loa. A road through desolate moonscape terrain, but
still, it would take him down into Hilo and then there'd be only another
twenty or so easier miles.

Would the young priest resent the imposition? Worry about his
parishioners, after all the rumors? But Father Huntly should have paid
a courtesy visit himself. Six months and not even a phone call. That

was wrong. Don't let niggling details get in the way of the big things, Father Huntly. Don't let them consume you. Don't, please, become a small-minded fussbudget.

After watching the sunset, he was ready, once more, to begin.

. . . I drove out to Tomas's place straight from the airport. The path through the jungle was the same, all those big trees wrapped in vines. A few anthurium and poinsettia still grew among the woods and high grass, and pandanus, banana, papaya, and mango trees were making an advance on the house. The vegetable beds had disappeared, and the double row of palms, heavy with dead fronds, rose up out of the weedy undergrowth like the bones of an ancient city. The place had a ghostly quality, abandoned on one level but not another.

Tomas was lying in a bedroom furnished only with a bed and small table, a tapa *cloth on one wall, and a* lahala *mat on the floor. He seemed terribly small under the sheet, and it scared me to find him like that in mid-afternoon. He awoke and showed little surprise at seeing me, the invader, in his house. I became acutely conscious of how the air around him remained undisturbed.*

Without a word he got up and went out to the lanai, and I followed. I could smell a flower that reminded me of gardenias; it brought back a memory of how I'd once given a corsage to a young lady and then spent the long humid evening inhaling that other-worldly fragrance. Now, too, that fragrance seemed to hint of another world just beyond our senses. It gave me hope. Tomas sat on the couch, slumped against it, as if the little walk from bedroom to lanai had tired him out. I took my chances and sat down next to him.

"You know, Tomas, I grew up on a farm,
too. On the mainland." I was scared, you see, to start right off the bat with Michael and so just jumped in anywhere. "Two of my brothers are running it now. The other's in construction and doing well for himself. My father's more or less retired. Less rather than more. He's still the boss." Thin ice! I realized too late. A farm. Sons. Good Lord, how stupid could I be! But I had to keep going to get out of it, and so briefly described the farm.

"What crops?" Tomas asked.

"*Not crops for selling, but for the dairy cows. Hay, and corn for silage. Alfalfa. All for the cows.*"

"*How many?*"

"*How many cows? A hundred and fifty it used to be. I'm not sure about now.*"

"*Lots of work, yeah?*"

"*Lots of work! Right! My father would never leave the place. Not even for a weekend. Oh, once he did. He took my mother on a little trip, and that was it for the next twenty years.*" I relived my old astonishment that anyone could live like that, walking the same—usually muddy—path from back porch to barn day in and day out. For a lifetime. A treadmill. But I also recalled how nice the big barn looked with its row of windows all yellow and steamy against the blue snow at dusk. I'm thinking that the greatest craving of youth—one of them anyway—is for the unknown and its challenge. So we quickly reject what's easily attainable. Oh, why? Who plays such tricks? Is it evolution driving us onward? Shaping some pattern, some design we can't yet see?

A shower passed, one of those brief cloudbursts I'd come to love, and I asked myself why that wasn't enough, the scent of rain, that miracle, the sweetness of plumeria, and the heated earth releasing its fragrance. Why must we have more? Isn't He present in a single raindrop? Or is that heresy, too? Pantheism. But still. If in a single raindrop, what of an entire shower!

I had to leave the farm, I told Tomas. I felt that my life wasn't there. It's something you know, but don't know how you know. "*But now,*" I said, "*I don't know anything!*" Tangled, confusing words, and tangled thoughts driving them—appalling, but I couldn't stop. "*They say you're a priest, too, Tomas. Then maybe you can understand what I'm trying to say. Tomas— I broke your flashlight that time I came to see you. I got lost on the way to the road and was so upset because I felt only fear inside me and nothing else. I thought you might have set the whole thing up, but that's OK. That doesn't matter now. What matters is—*" I smacked my chest hard. "*Still. Nothing much under the old hood!*"

I know I probably said a whole lot more, going on and on about the church reforms meant to bring about a great renewal of faith but unsettling me all the more. The new liturgy and new hymns that seemed, oh, too secular, too folksy. "*I have to start over somehow, Tomas. Get back to* the beginning." When there was no more I could say, I leaned back into a quiet as soothing as a bath.

Tomas shifted on the couch and I thought he was going to ask me to leave now. I'd talked way too much and not about Michael at all. But then he took a flattened cigarette from his pocket, tore it in two, and offered me half. I'd never smoked before, but that night did my best. I remember the ragged tip flaring like a Fourth of July sparkler when he lit it with a kitchen match.

It was dark by then, and Tomas went into the house and came out with a lighted lantern. Was he going to walk me back out to the road this time? He went down to the cinder drive, and I followed, again. But then he stopped and began pulling weeds that were nearly as tall as he was. Good Lord, I thought, he's gone mad. I started weeding, too, thinking that he would chase me away any minute, and I'd probably have to ask him for the lantern. But he kept working fast and didn't speak.

"Tomas," I said after a while, "I could send some boys over to help you get all this straightened around." The idea had come all at once, and I was pretty excited about it. With a little help, Tomas could put the grounds to rights in a few days maybe.

"I have a son," he said.

After that, I was afraid to say anything at all. We worked I don't know how long weeding that drive, moving the lantern ahead every so often and working toward the circle of light. Palm fronds clattered in a mild breeze, and I seemed to have more pep than I'd had in months. We stacked dead fronds in a big pile when the drive was clear, and then Tomas sat back on his heels and had another cigarette. There we were, hunched down in a bit of light. It struck me how lonely he must be—and maybe that was the reason he'd put up with me for so long.

"Tomas," I said. "Come to Honolulu with me. Michael's there. Let's visit him." Would he be mad at me because I knew Michael's where-abouts and maybe he didn't?

"Tomas? What do you think? Doesn't that sound like a good idea?"

He left me with the lantern and went into the house. I waited for at least half an hour out there, and when he didn't come out again, I thought, OK. Done is done. I tried. What more can a person do? I took the lantern and this time paid close attention to where I was going.

Later, as I thought about Tomas's odd silence, I decided that he simply needed time to think about it. I wouldn't rush him. So I stayed away. That was a mistake. Because I didn't go round to the village shops for a few days, I didn't learn right away about Roberto collapsing one night while making bread and then being taken to the hospital in Hilo. Mrs. Hakutani, who has the grocery across the road from Roberto's, told me that the next day Tomas had come into the village as usual and found the bakery closed. She had to go across the road to tell him what happened. Tomas went home, she said, and then they didn't see him around at all. I bought some groceries and went out to his house. He was in bed again, and this time appeared to be very ill.

"I brought you some fresh milk, Tomas. Would you like some, maybe warmed up?" I'd remembered to buy honey to sweeten it. Those small pains were starting and I prayed that the short-circuiting would hold off for just a while longer. I'd been in countless sickrooms and now waited for that other, professional self to take over, but that self was in hiding. I was scared and shaky and worried that I myself might pass out and then where would we be? As I heated the milk, an idea came to me. Why couldn't the parish pay off those liens? An emergency donation, I could say. Some mission inundated by a flood. Then I could reimburse the parish little by little—as I did, finally.

After drinking the milk, Tomas seemed stronger. He reached under his pillow and brought out a color photograph. It was of himself and Roberto on the bench outside the bakery. Tomas was grinning at the camera. The baker was saying something to Tomas but looked a little cranky, as he usually does. Tomas had on his green thongs, and his feet were crossed at the ankles. How many times had I seen him sitting this way!

"From Ohio," Tomas said. He pronounced it O-hee-o, and at first I thought he was saying something about the Hawaiian tree, the ohi'a, *which resembles a poplar.*

"This? Someone took this picture of you and Roberto? Someone from Ohio?"

Tomas nodded. He took back the photograph and looked at it for a long time. He touched Roberto's face, then put the photo back under the pillow and closed his eyes. "They have snow there," he said, just before dozing off.

Later I'd learn he'd been fasting and praying for Roberto, and that was why he was so weak. Delirious. I think he may have thought, at moments, that I was Michael, for at one point he urged me to lean close and then told me what I should do with his body when he died. I was to put it in some cave in a cliff above the ocean. Judging from his fragmented instructions, it would be a perilous affair. Roberto, I gathered, had agreed to do this, but now there was only me.

General weakness and a touch of malnutrition, our local doctor said. I shouldn't worry. Tomas would pull through. He needed rest and good food, that's all. Juana came from Honolulu to stay with him, but Michael was off somewhere on Maui and she hadn't been able to reach him. I didn't tell her what Tomas had said about dying and the cave burial and all. In the next nights my dreams were awful. I'd see the landmarks he'd described—the ironwood pines and black cliffs—and I'd see Tomas sliding down the cliff into the sea, and I'd feel myself slipping, losing hold, and plunging into surging white water.

I'd wake up all sweaty and wonder if Tomas had known it was me he was talking to and not Michael. Had known, but asked me all the same. If so, why? Did he want to get back at me somehow? Did he want to nullify what he thought was my power, or think he could? I wracked my brain trying to figure it out when I should have been looking to the heart. Maybe Tomas just wanted what he wanted, and since I was there, caring for him . . . But if he had cursed me—chills and fear came again—why would he ask me to do such an important thing? Me, of all people. In the end I decided I'd do whatever Tomas asked of me, curse or no. It would be my last chance to make amends. Again, the irony of this!

Juana stayed for over a week but had to leave on a trip for the museum. Tomas was eating pretty well by then and sleeping better. I saw no reason why she shouldn't leave for a few days. I could stay with him. It bothered me, though, that he didn't recognize her at times and called her by his wife's name. I should have trusted my instincts. Soon after Juana left, he had a relapse. At one point when he seemed very bad, he started chanting rhythmical fragments in Hawaiian. He was praying, I knew. I did as well, in my beloved Latin.

"It's time," he murmured. I talked to him. I put cool cloths on his forehead—anything to keep him here. Finally he opened his eyes. He seemed very sad, as if a bad trick had been played on him. When he grew a little stronger, he asked for paper and pencil and laboriously printed, One acre, Roberto Malacha. Eight acre Michael Koe and Juana Koe. One acre, the priest. *He asked how to spell my name.*

I told him. The name sounded foreign even to me! I thought of my promise about the burial and worried I'd never be able to go through with it. Another betrayal. Nor did I want any more of Tomas's land now. How could I accept it in good conscience? As for the burial, I was plain scared. I'd heard enough about Island practices to know that anything having to do with secret caves was dangerous business—not because of the caves so much, though they were often booby-trapped with poisons, but because of the living guardians of those caves. There's a word, Kapu! which means Keep Out! Forbidden! *I had no business at all in someone's secret cave, but here was Tomas, formalizing that promise. I told him again what the doctor had said, that he was going to get better. I said we no longer needed the land; he might consider giving a little more to Roberto, or to Michael and Juana. I tried a joke.* "Tomas," *I said,* "look at me. How can I go climbing cliff trails and what not? I'm not the right person for that kind of stuff! And what about Roberto? He's better now."*

I think he recognized the fear under my words. Smiling, he said, "You."

I had one last card and decided to play it. "Then what about our trip to Honolulu? What about seeing Michael in Honolulu?"

Tomas turned to the window and stared out at a large tree netted with wood-rose vines. It was nearly sunset, and the tree appeared to be covered with strings of yellow lights. He nodded, and then got better by the hour.

The priest rubbed his sore fingers, swollen now, and decided to nap a bit before continuing. But as he lay on the couch in his study, he couldn't shake the thought that someone was watching him. On the edge of sleep, he'd pull back, alarmed, and opening his eyes, would see only the lighted room, his desk, the papers all over it, and once the cat sleeping there. Images of Honolulu kept flickering, a movie skidding forward and back. He was suddenly afraid this was it—the film would snap this time and the screen go dark for good. He got up and made himself a cup of instant coffee and carried it back to the study.

. . . A few weeks later we were on our way. As the plane took off, Tomas closed his eyes and clutched the basket of treats for his children,

*fancy Puna papayas, loaves of Roberto's sweet-bread, and dried fish deli-
cacies from Mrs. Hakutani. The plane roared and shook, and there was
Tomas, his eyes squeezed shut, his body rigid. I couldn't believe how
stupid I'd been. The trip would be too much for him—for me, too. He
relaxed, though, when the plane leveled, and I told him he could have a
cigarette if he wanted, and even some juice or a drink. Tomas didn't
want a thing. He could hardly bring himself to look away from the
window even though it was dark and there was nothing to see but the
airplane's flashing light on the wingtip. Was he thinking about his
ancestors crossing those waters in the dark, in long war canoes? A little
Japanese girl behind us kept pulling on the back of Tomas's seat and
chanting, "Ala-mo-ana." Her mother laughed and asked if she could say*
shopping. *The little girl only repeated her chant. It reminded me of a
Greek word,* alaomai, *which means* I wander, I am banished. *I told
Tomas this.*

"Ala-o-mai," *Tomas said.*

"That's right. And what does ala moana *mean, Tomas?"*

"Ocean way."

*Now it means, of course, a major Honolulu street and a large shop-
ping center.*

"Shop-ping!" we heard. *"Say* shop-ping.*"*

"Ala-mo-ana!"

*And then we were flying low, parallel to brilliant lights on the leeward
side of Oahu.*

*The crowded terminal, the taxi ride through the bright city, didn't
seem to faze Tomas, but he balked when we reached the courtyard gardens outside Juana's condominium. Somewhere people were having a
party. We heard laughter and could smell meat roasting. Tomas stopped
near a carp pool.*

"What's the matter, Tomas? Don't you feel good?"

He shook his head.

"Are you sick? Do you want to sit down for a while and rest?"

*He turned abruptly and began walking back the way we'd come. I had
to rush after him and grab his arm. Having him lost in the city was the
last thing I wanted then.*

"Tomas, tell me. What's the matter?"

He stood on the flagstone walk, taking in a narrow stream edged with stones, then a lava wall covered with pink and white orchids, then luxuriant green bedding plants strung with hooded lights.

"Who does this?" he said.

"What?" I looked around, trying to find the source of his unhappiness.

With his hand, he shaped the walkway and gardens, the stream and carp pool in the air, comparing this carefully landscaped courtyard, I realized, to his own overgrown land. My own hand swung into the air to shape a hurried answer. "Not one man, Tomas! Many! Many kanakas working hard." I went into a frenzy of motion, showing imaginary crews planting, watering, digging. "No one man can do this. No way."

Tomas sagged a little, but allowed me to lead him to an elevator. He became very quiet, dazed maybe, by still another miracle. Did he see it as all part of a magic he couldn't hope to create himself for his children? We walked along a balcony and came to Juana's door. Tomas stared bleakly at its rich wood grain as I rang the bell. Just as the door was opening, I slipped away. Tomas had to be alone with them, I thought, or all advantage would be lost in those first minutes. I saw his startled, panicky look in that fraction of a second before I moved away. I caught a glimpse of Juana, in white, with a spray of orchids in her hair. "You're here!" she said, embracing him. "I can't believe it!"

Down in the courtyard, I kept an eye on the elevator, prepared to run after Tomas if he appeared. When enough time passed, I went back up. Juana was smiling as she motioned toward the lanai. Tomas and Michael were out there, standing quite close to one another—dark shapes against the lights along the ridges of the mauka, or mountain, end of Honolulu. She had set her glass dining table with white plates, and there were white anthurium tipped with spring green in a glass bowl. Lighted candles, too. My legs gave out on me, and I was glad to fall back into a deep sofa. Juana's carpeting, I remember, was the color of beach sand, sugar sand, we used to say in Wisconsin, and the thought struck me: Where have we gotten to now?

The priest stood and walked stiffly into the kitchen to close Francis's window. He imagined he heard drums, many drums—wind sweeping up from the ocean, carrying the sound from the direction of Kawaihai.

"I'm not scared, Tomas," he said. "I've made pretty good headway, and even if I should go tonight, Kani can take what's there to Father Huntly—for better or worse, hey?" He laughed. His voice, the laughter, sounded nutty to him, a crazy man talking and laughing to himself. Good Lord. But there were drums, no question. He listened intently. And chanting. He was sure of it.

FIVE

The next morning, to celebrate his survival and to reestablish connection with the human community, he decided to drive into Kailua and take care of a number of errands. It cheered him that he'd been right about the drums and chanting—Kani telling him that morning about the big luau at the Mauna Kea the previous night. So he wasn't, he told himself, nutsy-cuckoo, not yet. And Tomas was hardly haunting him.

The road to Kailua wound through a desert of smooth and rough lava fields covered here and there with clumps of long grass. To his left he could see darkened areas spilling down the flanks of Hualalai. These flows had inundated most of the white sand beaches in the area, sparing a few green and white crescents. But to get to them, people had to take four-wheel-drives over nearly invisible trails indicated by no more than a lighter, more powdery gray through the arid terrain. Passing this way, the priest was always tempted to try. How nice to see, he imagined. At one faint track, he braked, then warned himself not to be goofy. He sped up again, driving toward pools of illusory water pouring over the highway, the landscape silver and black. He might have been, he thought, on the back of a surfacing whale.

He passed tourists pulled over to the side, building small pyramids of lava stones or printing their names on the dark lava with bits of bleached coral used in the roadbed, a favorite tourist pursuit in recent years. Both sides of the road were cluttered with these pyramids, some toppled, and with initials in stark white. He'd seen people knocking down monuments in order to build their own. Several miles later, a figure in the distance appeared to be doing exercises along the side of the road. It took a while for the priest to understand that he was being asked to stop. He braked hard, skidding onto the shoulder beyond the figure and a parked car, stalling the Toyota. Light-headed from the scare, he climbed out and walked back toward a small group, pushing himself through sunlight that took away his breath and then the day itself. He had to stop.

"You all right?" A man's voice.

"Oh yes, thank you." He waited for things to reassemble. Plaid bermudas, then short-sleeved shirt, a glare, then sunglasses and red nose. Bald, and no hat for protection. The man. Behind him, higher up on the lava field, a woman in halter and shorts. Two young boys, maybe ten and twelve. The woman was holding a piece of lava, ready to drop it into a cardboard box.

"You gotta jack in your car?" the man said. "Somebody musta stole the one from this piece of junk. Thank God there's a spare, though."

"Ah, I see—" What? Everything slipped his mind, and they were all waiting. The woman's skin rosy even in the bleaching light.

"You have a Toyota, too, so maybe your jack'll work. Cripes, that's all we needed, I thought, in this godforsaken place. We're supposed to be back in Hilo tonight."

When the priest didn't respond, the man added, "How about if I just check your trunk? You might want to sit down for a while."

"Oh no, but you go right ahead. I'm fine. I hope I have one."

While the man worked at changing the tire, the woman, still up on the lava field, asked the priest where he was from, "back in the States."

"Originally Wisconsin, but I, ah, live here now."

"*You* do. No kidding."

The priest had on khaki slacks and an aloha shirt patterned with State of Hawaii flags and with Nene geese, an indigenous, endangered species. He'd plastered his pink flaking skin with sunscreen, and zinc oxide coated his nose. A yellow terry-cloth hat drooped low over his forehead. He supposed they took him for a liar. Those boys in their T-shirts and cutoffs, their skin a gleaming brown, looked more like *kamaiinas,* or locals, than he ever could.

"I live just up the road. Lived on this island for, oh, forty-some years now." He flipped up his collar against the sun.

"*Really.* Then maybe you know of a good place to eat in Kailua? Someplace you don't have to dress up?"

He told them about his favorite restaurant near the pier, where excellent Chinese food was served at reasonable prices. Giving directions, he repeated himself several times and waved his arms as if blessing the lava fields.

"Great!" the man said, interrupting. "Well, gang, I guess that's *it*. We were lucky." He twitched his head in the direction of the boys, who moved toward the Toyota. "There's a lot we wanted to see yet." He took the jack to the priest's car.

In her wedgies, the woman lurched over the broken terrain and stumbled down to the shoulder. She kicked the box of lava chunks. "Souvenirs," she said. "I don't know how the heck we'll get them back. On the plane, I suppose." She turned to her sons. "That's enough, boys. I said no *more*."

"Excuse me," the priest said, "but I don't think you should, ah, take the stones. They're—"

"Oh, but look how many there are! A zillion. I can't see where taking a couple of rocks is going to hurt anything. You know something? That's what I don't understand. The . . . oh, possessiveness here. Well, maybe I do. What would happen if we all took bits of paradise home with us, hey? Then there'd be no more left for you guys. Right? Boys, in the car. They say they want tourists, and yet—"

"Maureen," the man said.

"It's just—" the priest began. "I mean, they might be, ah, sacred."

"You're kidding," the woman said. The boys hefted the box into the backseat and got in.

"Thanks for the restaurant tip," the man said. "Maureen? ready?"

"Wait a sec. What do you mean, sacred? I mean, they go and build a road through here, right over all this stuff. Is the road sacred, too? Maybe we shouldn't even be driving on it, hey?"

"Maureen."

"Oh no, not the road, no. The thing is, stones from *heiau* sites are sacred, and a person never knows where the old sites might have been. Some are known, of course, but not all, and so, in any case, it's best not to take any stones. You can get hurt, you see."

"Really? How, hurt?"

"Well—" He glanced at her high wedgies and sunburned feet. "Foot injuries, for example. There've been a lot of those. Falls. Broken legs. Strange accidents." He explained how, each year, the park service people received boxes of rocks mailed back, with apologies, from places all over the mainland.

"Hey, that's pretty exciting. Boys, you listening?" They were giggling in the backseat, ducking their heads below the window.

"I'm a priest, you see, a Catholic priest. I'm not at all sure about this, either, but—"

"A priest? You're kidding."

"Well, thanks a lot. Again," the man said. "We really have to get going."

"Also," the priest went on quickly—they were backing away from him—"it may be best not to travel with, ah, pork of any kind in the car, especially on the other side of the island."

They had stopped and were staring at him now, and suddenly he was in the middle of a sermon he'd once given—on Madame Pele and the intertwining of Christian and Hawaiian beliefs. It felt good to be talking again, the words just coming, the ideas, the connections always raising goose bumps.

"Right," the man said, when the priest paused. "We'll keep that in mind."

"Ah, where you folks from, on the mainland?"

"Buffalo," the woman said. "And we gotta go back tomorrow, darn it. So we're kind of in a rush, you know? Have to drive all the way to Hilo tonight."

"Ah. Buffalo. I've never been there, myself. I imagine it's quite cold there. You read—"

"Well, it's actually June there now, as well. So, not too bad."

Screeches came from the rocking car.

He let them get a head start and then followed more slowly in the Toyota. By the time he reached the airport outside Kailua, he didn't feel quite so idiotic, and there were fine shrubs of bougainvillea to look at. Planted along both sides of the road, the sprays of magenta and yellow-gold formed a festive barrier against the black plain, a kind of triumphal entryway into the village. He found it hard to keep his eyes on the road.

While the Toyota had an oil change and tune-up, he ate an early supper of Chinese food at the restaurant near the pier, keeping an eye out for the family he'd met. A marlin tournament was in progress and the restaurant crowded, but no one seemed to recognize him. He felt comfortably anonymous, almost a tourist himself. He finished his meal quickly—others were waiting for his table—then walked along the harbor front, avoiding the excitement at the end of the pier, where fishermen were posing for pictures alongside a huge, prehistoric-looking creature winched up on chains. From the narrow harbor beach came the smell of marijuana. The main street, where Hawaiian royalty once rode in their carriages, was bumper to bumper with traffic. Tourists in bright outfits, some a bit too scanty, the priest thought, jammed the sidewalks, which fronted shops selling coral jewelry, resort attire, macadamia nuts and candies, Kona coffee, trinkets, and luxury items of all kinds. At the village bookstore, he bought a two-day-old *New York Times,* glancing without much comprehension at headlines having to do with the Palestinians. Back outside, he walked with an unusually peppy stride, the paper tucked under one arm. Out on the bay, a powerboat zoomed toward the open ocean, launching a parachuted water-skier high above the water. The priest watched for a long time, trying to imagine it. Then it was time to get the Toyota. His driver's license no longer permitted night driving.

He didn't wait for the next morning. By eight that evening he was back in his study, pen refilled, papers rearranged, and cat eyeing him, crouched at one corner of the desk. The priest picked up a smooth oval lava stone from the desk and held it against his face a moment, then was writing.

. . . A few years later, Father Huntly, Roberto came for me in his old station wagon. I'd been digging in a lettuce bed behind the rectory and stopped only to wash my hands and grab, out of habit, the kit for the Last Sacrament I always kept on the hall table. "It's time," Roberto said. I was so surprised, then, to find Tomas sitting in his living room as if waiting for a bus. His white shirt was clean and pressed. So were his khaki slacks. What's going on? I wanted to ask, but their solemnity made it clear that I was only an acolyte in their ritual. Roberto brought a garden cart around to the lanai *and helped Tomas into it, and then we pulled him down the cinder drive and under the big trees to the car. I tried to think, in vain, of something to say that would stop the crazy business. Tomas didn't at all seem like a dying man. At the end of the path Roberto turned the car around so Tomas could look at his land one last time.*

We drove down through new papaya plantations, then through a stretch of volcanic rubble and cinder cones where the village of Kapoho used to be. The ocean just beyond was a long bar of light. Closer to sea level, the road narrowed into a single lane cutting through jungle. After a few miles Roberto turned off at random, it seemed, and drove through a stand of ironwood pines, the car bumping over lava stones and tree roots. And then there were the cliffs—black and shiny, as in my dreams years ago. Roberto parked, and we helped Tomas out. The car doors slamming seemed too loud in that breezy quiet. A holy place, I sensed at once, though eerie in its remoteness. Waves thudded against the cliffs, sending up explosions of spray. It seemed a miracle the cliffs remained intact. Roberto brought mats from the trunk and unrolled them far enough away from the edge so we wouldn't get wet from the spray. I was scared. Were we supposed to put him in some cave as he was? Leave him there? I wouldn't do it. Nor would I let Roberto do it, no matter what Tomas said. Waves were slamming away forty feet below us, regularly as a tolling bell.

On the other side of the island the sun was setting. Tourists were aiming cameras and taking pictures. Here, there was just a gradual falling off of light, and the air cooling. On the horizon, clouds were turning pale rose over gray water. Salt mist from the crashing waves drifted up, often hanging in the air like a veil or a shroud. I could taste the salt on my lips. I'd heard the stories—how that whole area, so remote, was the sanctuary of Hawaiian ghosts biding their time. It's one thing to hear such stories and think, oh, there always are stories like that, but quite another to actually be in such a place after sunset, with two people who were acting so detached and strange. Every so often Roberto would pluck a stem of grass and chew it, avoiding my eyes. He seemed to be waiting for something— a signal?—from Tomas, but Tomas sat looking out over the water, his knees drawn up and his arms linked around them. A double-masted sailboat appeared, heading south. Tomas went to the cliff edge to watch it. Like the sails, his shirt and white hair glowed in the remaining light. I wanted to warn him—my dream again—but their manner, everything, seemed to forbid speech. When the sailboat moved out of sight, Tomas came back and lay down. Roberto threw his stem of grass away and found a new one. I could hardly bear the deliberation of all this, their silence, those waves thudding, and so went to the car for my kit. But of course Tomas had never been baptized, to my knowledge. Before the Last

Sacrament, I'd have to administer the first. I chastized myself for not having done this when he had been so sick that time.

"Tomas? May I baptize you?"

He shook his head. I looked at Roberto, who also shook his head. Near
the cliff edge was a small pool of water. I braved the edge, scooped some
up, and returned to Tomas. But I let it run through my fingers into the
pine needles. God forgive me, but how could I disobey a dying man's
wish? Betray him again? I hedged my bets, though, by clutching the vial
of oil I'd brought and saying the words of the Last Sacrament to myself.
Tomas opened his eyes and looked at me as if he knew.

It grew darker and damp. Roberto went to the car for blankets. I
wrapped up and watched the moon sliding up from the ocean like some
new continent. The big waves had a glassy sheen to them, then would
come the thud, and spray drifting up in moonlight.

"John," Tomas said. He'd never used my name before. My heart was
going to town.

"Yes, Tomas?"

"You no malihini."

Stranger. I touched his shoulder. "No," I said. "Not now."

"You no kolea ino."

Again I said no, but this time in ignorance. I thought of my father, as
he'd been before his illness. A solid oak beam of a man. My mother said
he was terribly wasted at the end. I wouldn't have recognized him. He'd
lost most of his hair from chemotherapy, and new hair, fine as duck
down, had just been growing in. His face and head, my mother said, still
caught in the shock of it, seemed just like an infant's. His eyes, too. I saw
this when I went back—that transcendent gaze, that preoccupation with
another world.

Now I was looking at Tomas in the moonlight—half the size of the
man I'd first known. His head seemed enlarged by contrast. Half a million years for this miracle of evolution! Surely there must be a reason for
that great development. Nature is functional. Waste, yes. Spoilage and
rot and disease, yes. But also form and function. What is it we're supposed to see with these complex mechanisms?

"Forgive me," I heard Tomas say. My heart thudded in echo to those
waves. Why? What had he done? An image of Tomas and Roberto on the

bench, laughing to themselves, came to me, and now here we were, in this remote spot.

"Yes," I said, and added to myself, for whatever. *Lord forgive me, but I was scared and didn't trust Roberto at all.* "And will you forgive me, Tomas?"

He didn't respond, and I thought, then he won't. He can't. But he opened his eyes finally and took something from his pocket. A cigarette, I thought, remembering that night. But it was a stone, a pocked lava stone, smooth and warm. Gray in the moonlight. He gave it to me. I think it might be from the great heiau at Kawaihai, where his ancestor had been a temple priest.

Then Tomas slept. I tried to tell myself he was getting better and we'd go back soon. But Roberto didn't move; Tomas didn't move, and gradually I accepted the idea that we would be there to the end. Wind came up, bringing a shower. We covered Tomas and sat huddled under blankets. I watched clouds part and the moon appear lower in the southwest. There were a few dim stars, constellations whose names I'd never learned. I thought of the Polynesians guided by the stars to a landing not far from these cliffs, with their gods wrapped carefully in leaves and cloth for the journey. I dozed off and when I awoke at one point and looked at Tomas in the moonlight, wrapped for his own journey, I knew he'd already left us. I spent the time until dawn praying.

The night paled, the cliffs reappeared, and the pines beaded with rain, and on the horizon a line of fire suddenly shot out toward us, forming a path across the water. In this new light I could see that Roberto had been weeping. His face was puffy and haggard, sullen. Tomas's head was turned away from us and toward the sun.

"Take off your shoes," Roberto said.

I wasn't scared now. A death can do that—puts the self in its place and silences its whining demands and self-centered fears. Waves were breaking against the cliff almost gently, and the ocean was becoming that deep sapphire I'd seen from the deck of the ship so long ago, its white water tinted aqua as in very wet, pure snow. I felt becalmed and numb. If he wants to push me over the cliff, I thought crazily, well OK. Here I am.

Roberto apparently did not wish to murder me, at least not then. He motioned me to help him lift Tomas's body, and then we negotiated a trail along the cliff face, a trail only inches wide in places. I tried not to *think too much about the waves and those lava boulders and spikes, but concentrated on placing my feet, white and ludicrous and totally unsuited for what I was asking them to do. There were sharp stones and the path was often slippery. At one point, it dropped down quite close to the water. During high tides, the trail must be submerged. When was the next tide? Soon we began ascending and the trail widened. There were small shrubs growing along the edge, and roots provided footholds. I relaxed a bit, but at the mouth of the cave, all but hidden by a shrub, my legs, already weak, nearly buckled under me. There, on rows of trestles disappearing in the dimness, were dozens of coffins. The ones nearest the opening were falling apart with the damp. Roberto gave me wordless instructions, and we left the light for that gloom. I signaled Roberto to wait; I couldn't see anything at first. When my eyes adjusted, we carried Tomas's body down an aisle and placed it in a tapa-lined coffin that looked newly made. The wood was dark and oily. Possibly koa. The tapa cloth lining it was from Tomas's bedroom, I'm sure. In the shadows along the wall were calabashes and gourds and even a small canoe. I could see a dusty spear and a drum. Tomas was going home.*

The sun was fully up when we reached the top of the cliff. Roberto waved to two fishermen out on a spire of lava beyond the white water and connected to the cliff by a narrow, winding causeway. They waved back. To get out there they had to be agile as tightrope walkers—and just as daring. I don't think they were there to fish.

I was glad enough to sit down and rest, while Roberto smoked a cigarette, staring out over the water. I wondered if those men worried him. I said a few silent prayers for Tomas and recited to myself fragments from the Requiem Mass. May light eternal shine upon Tomas Koe, O Lord, with Thy saints forevermore. For Thou art gracious— Eternal rest give him, O Lord, and let perpetual light shine upon him, for Thou art gracious— *Then I just sat there. Sunlight struck me. Salt mist. Wind seemed to blow right through me, through an emptiness almost peace.*

"Father," Roberto said, "will you say some words?"

It took a while for this to register, and when I understood what he wanted, I crawled upright and on tottery legs went to the very edge where Tomas had stood. Hair at the back of my neck prickled. Would it be now?—the push? I raised my arms in the direction of the watchful fishermen, and words—Latin words—formed on their own: In principio erat Verbum et Verbum erat apud Deum, et Deus erat Verbum—*The*

beginning of the Holy Gospel according to St. John swelling outward . . .
et lux in tenebris lucet, et tenebrae eam non comprehenderunt—
Light in light and the darkness grasping it not.

And that was how, Father Huntly, our new parish building came to be named St. Thomas Hall.

The old priest looked up at the morning—his scrubby garden taking shape, the hillside and sea forming once again.

SIX

On the front seat of the Toyota, the manila envelope holding his letter; a map of the Big Island folded to show the Saddle Road; his lunch of cheese sandwiches, grapefruit juice, and bananas. In a duffel bag in back, his pills, a few items of clothing, his breviary, and three one-pound cans of Kona coffee. Also a flashlight in case he should get stranded somewhere up on the flank of Mauna Kea. In the kitchen, a note for Kani. What had he forgotton?

Nothing. He was all set. The thought gave him a little boost as he drove through grassy lava fields. He could still remember things, function as other people did! He wasn't washed up, not yet. And he'd gotten through the writing, imagine. That was why, he thought now, he'd felt so much like doing something, just going, the momentum still there, inside him. The road turned southeast, and he could see burnt-sienna rocks strewn about—holding minerals galore, he'd read, and straight from the center of the earth, cast up by lava but too heavy to be carried to the sea. Sunlight turned the lava fields into glaring lakes. Ahead, the road seemed to melt. Ten miles further upslope, he was in gray-green scrub. He imagined Kani finding his note and half-expected to see one of her sons tearing up behind him in a rattletrap. But no cars came up from behind. No cars passed in the opposite direction, heading down to Waikoloa, the golf oasis hidden in scrub. The road leveled a bit, and he eased the straining Toyota into third. Enough power? It seemed OK. He stuck his elbow out the window, then withdrew it at once. Too hot.

He wished Kani were with him. She might be able to tell him things about this and that, as she often did. But she didn't have time to go gallivanting around. This he knew, yet imagined the fuss such a thing might cause in Pahoa, should word get around. He had to smile. But he was lonely—all part and parcel of it, maybe, the mystery of priesthood. And maybe one way of tricking those molecules into new configurations, if only for a second or two. The Toyota had no radio, but the priest didn't mind. He sang every stanza of the "Tantum Ergo" aloud, in Latin, happy in the remembering.

Near the top of the Saddle Road he came to a somnolent army camp base with abrasive turquoise fuel tanks and rows of sheet-metal quonset huts. Just beyond was a deserted-looking state park area, where he stopped to give the Toyota a rest. A few log cabins for hunters and hikers blended with the russet, gray-green landscape. Near one cabin a car, but no one was about. The air was thin and much cooler. He took several deep breaths, imagining a brilliant fall morning after a heavy frost.

At a picnic table he had one of his sandwiches, then took a walk along the row of cabins, each with its stack of chopped firewood. It felt good to walk after the tension of driving, and he wondered what it would be like to be a real hiker. Beyond the cabins he came to a trail that would take him higher up Mauna Kea. On either side were the mineralized rocks, configured like petrified skulls. Large black flies, warmed to life by the hot sun, droned circles around him. *Kiawe* trees twisted toward the earth, their small leaves dried and withered. He wished he had an index card. He wanted to remember a particular clump of gray grass bearing two seed fronds for this moonscape terrain. At a barbed-wire fence with a gate left ajar, something was stretched across the top wire, a brown rag of a thing he recognized, after a moment, as a carcass with the head—mostly skull—still attached. His heart stopped, then pounded on. The place suddenly frightened him—death everywhere in the silence. Walking faster, he tried meditating on the big telescopes mounted on the summit of Mauna Kea, some six thousand feet higher up, in snow and sometimes great winds. Massive reflecting mirrors. Wondrous hexagon mosaics drawing scientists closer and closer to First Light, deeper into Mystery.

—Imagine, Tomas. While down here we're still fooling around with bingo and million dollar jackpots.

This thought made him angry. Here he was, wandering about, when he should be talking to Father Huntly! He spun around and hurried back but found himself sliding down into a gulch littered with the skull rocks and white, glittering chips. Bone fragments, he realized, and there a jawbone with crumbling teeth. A shattered tusk. A wild boar run, clearly. He imagined one of the creatures suddenly bursting through the scrub behind him, small stones flying from its sharp hooves, its razors slicing the air, him.

He grappled for holds, trying to climb out, but a thudding blast knocked him back down. The noise was heavy and full and rounded, and the aftermath stillness reverberated with it. A *kiawe* branch swished down, striking him on the shoulder, but he felt nothing. A second blast, encompassing everything, it seemed, pitched him forward into the dirt and bone fragments. In the moment before blacking out, he sensed chutes opening underneath him, opening onto the center of the earth.

Then, inexplicably, he was standing at the Toyota's door, a *kamai-ina* hunter holding it open for him. Sky, earth, scrub, and rocks all appeared metallic in the bronze light and much colder air. "You coulda froze out there, man!" the hunter was saying.

"I'm on medications," the priest tried to say, though his face hurt when he spoke. "I must have fallen asleep."

"Yeah? Well, take care of yourself. Maybe don't go off on your own no more, eh?"

The priest gave the hunter a can of Kona coffee and weakly climbed into the car. He couldn't shake the fright of dreaming his death and finding nothing there, in the lightless cave of the skull rocks, nothing at all.

Descending the mountain, he tried to fight despair by focusing on the work at hand and planning a lighthearted greeting. I hope you'll let me stay the night! I'm illegal, you know, driving after dark! But the young man who answered the door at the rectory in Pahoa appeared to be a stranger, in faded Levi's and a gray sweatshirt with cutoff sleeves. He was very tan. He was barefoot. And his white hair, more like fleece, was impossibly curled. Father Huntly's brother?

"Is, ah, Father Huntly here?"

"*I'm* Father Huntly! And you're— I know you somehow, don't I?"

"I was, ah, pastor—"

"Father LaClaire! Gosh, I'm really sorry. C'mon in!"

A stylish rattan couch and chairs replaced the old furniture in the living room. A woven rug in natural straw gave the room a faint smell of hemp. There was a new TV and a stereo cabinet. Handsome chrome bookcases. But the Pope's picture was where it had always been. And the Blessed Virgin's. This gave the priest hope.

"That's quite a scrape you've got. Did you just do it? I've got some good stuff. You don't want it getting infected."

"Oh, please, don't bother—" But Father Huntly had already left the room. Just give him the letter, he told himself, then say he had to get back. Sleep in the car, maybe. Somewhere. When Father Huntly returned, the older priest was sunk in oatmeal-colored cushions; he couldn't remember sitting down. One side of his face felt numb.

"Here you go. But I'd wash that cut out good first. Looks like there's dirt in it. Why don't you do that, and I'll find us something to eat. Tomorrow's shopping day. There's not much here, I'm afraid. I've got some herbal tea, though, and also decaf."

"A little milk?"

"Oh, sure! Milk, I have. Right." He rushed away.

The old priest wondered what if he'd said Jameson's instead. He wished he had. From the bathroom he could smell bread being toasted. Roberto's?

It was. With strawberry jam.

"You're looking at my hair, aren't you?" Father Huntly said.

"No." A lie.

"It's OK. Everybody does at first. My one great vanity. *This*, I'm ashamed to say—" He pulled a curl taut. "—is a permanent, would you believe. Never again. It's caused more grief and more talk than—" He rubbed his nearly white moustache. "Well. You can imagine."

"Than I did?"

Father Huntly laughed, flushing. The old priest imagined him on a surfboard.

"Can you believe it? I mean, on the mainland it would be no big deal."

"It's . . . striking."

"For sure. But really, it's a problem. I had no *idea*— I've heard, well, you can guess. I was thinking I should have it straightened the next time I'm in Honolulu. But that might make it worse. Better to just let it grow out, maybe. Have it chopped off little by little and be done with it."

"I'm sorry."

"Me too! But hey. What about *you?* How've you been doing? I really apologize for not getting over there to see you. I really meant to, but got so caught up in things here. Getting things off the ground. We've got some new ministries now, and a youth group. And I've started some new fun things to bring people together more during the week. Tonight was our Night at the Races. It's great!" He took a pack of cigarettes from the TV. Do you smoke?"

"What races? Are there races now in Pahoa?"

This made Father Huntly laugh again. "Oh heavens! Hardly. Just on film. At the hall. We place small bets on horses just as if we were at a racetrack. People are wild about it. You should hear the cheering and hollering. We made enough this week for a new set of dishes for the hall. Eventually I'd like to remodel the kitchen out there. Um, you don't approve, do you? I can tell."

"No."

"I really don't think it's harmful. Everybody has a great time. It fosters a real sense of community and—"

"It's gambling. The people here have great fun at cockfights, too." That was a bit harsh.

"Oh, but not the same thing!"

"On Mauna Kea, Father Huntly—" He couldn't control his voice. It sounded as if he'd be bawling any minute. "Scientists are in awe. Reverent! They're becoming the new theologians, Father Huntly!" The tightness in his throat now. Oh, stop, he told himself, knowing he couldn't, the words coming. "They're not up there playing bingo or cards, or watching films of racing horses and placing bets. Nor are they playing guitars and singing insipid songs. The money they spend on their computers and laboratories is the equivalent of what we once spent on our cathedrals, Father Huntly! The Fermi lab, which I have seen—

"Oh, please. Things have to change. Change is necessary. We must work for change and not Adventures in Paradise raffles or whatever. I've written down some things which—" His face hurt, throbbing now with each word. "Here. Please. Take it and read it as soon as possible. I was going to send it but thought I should— Please. Take it."

Father Huntly, withdrawn and somber, took the packet, and the old priest realized he'd badly offended him. Go slower! "It's about what I did here," he said, trying to sound neutral. Conversational. "Some of the things anyway, and about Tomas Koe. Have you heard of him? No? Tomas Koe was a *kahuna*, a Hawaiian priest. Born in another time and place, he might have understood the telescopes, the computers. As it was, he had his chants and his faith, which I tried to, well, pretty much wreck for him—"

Father Huntly was standing now, envelope in hand and looking blankly at the stereo, not wanting eye contact, it seemed. Embarrassed, maybe, for him. The old priest heard a rush of wind and spattering of rain. He could smell plumeria. From the grove he'd planted.

—Oh, Tomas. Here I go again, messing everything up.

"You must be beat," Father Huntly said. "After your drive and all. The guest room's all set. You know where it is! Tomorrow after Mass, I'll show you some of the neat things we're doing around here. But get a good sleep. You'll feel a lot better in the morning."

"Thank you. That's very kind." But something was coming to mind. Something important—from another sermon he'd given, and now, again, needing to be said. "Do you know of Jean Nicolet, Father Huntly?"

"Is he a parishioner?"

"Oh no! He was an explorer. A *voyageur,* they were called in the seventeeth century. He very much wanted to find a route to China. One day, if I have the story right, after crossing a great body of water, he and his party came upon a group of natives and he got all excited. He'd brought special clothes with him and put them on—a long silk bathrobe sort of thing, and then went out waving his pistols in some great ceremonial display. The Indians didn't know what was going on, and after a while it began to dawn on Jean Nicolet that neither did he—"

"By the way, I meant to tell you there's a blanket in the bottom drawer in case—"

"The thing is, he's standing there, see, looking at the Indians—they were Winnebago Indians—and he's thinking, Where the heck *am* I? I'm somewhere, but *where?*"

"That's quite a story. How about another glass of milk before you—"

"It's the explorer's *true* vision, Father Huntly!"

"Yes. I see. Well, I'd better say good night and let you get some rest. Tomorrow afternoon I have to go into Hilo, but there's nothing on right after Mass. We'll be able to have a nice breakfast and chat some more then. When did you say you were leaving?"

Chat. Father Huntly humoring him—an old man on the brink. It was hard to fall asleep. His face hurt, and words were still coming. All the crazy ones he'd said, and all those he hadn't.

Later that night, searching for the bedside lamp, which failed to materialize, he bumped something and heard a dreamy, tinkling crash. Nor was the wall light switch where it should have been. Then he bumped his shin hard against a piece of furniture.

Not in Wisconsin, he thought, but in South Kohala, on the leeward side of the island of Hawaii, called the Big Island, the youngest inhabited island in the Hawaiian archipelago. Honolulu, the principal city, is located on the island of Oahu, northwest of the island of Hawaii, and is some two thousand nautical miles from San Francisco.

But where was his desk?

His hands brushed circles against the wall until he came to curtains, then draw cords. A little light entered. And there was the light switch, on the opposite wall.

Not in South Kohala, he realized, but in Puna—that's where he was. In the guest room at the rectory that had been his home for forty years. And Father Huntly, who looked like a *haole* surfer, was now pastor. Whereas he was a guest and had broken a glass. Stepped on some.

With his handkerchief he mopped up broken glass and water, then shook fragments noisily into a wastebasket. He wiped up a few spots of blood, made the bed, and found his duffel bag. Downstairs, he placed two cans of Kona coffee on the kitchen table, but then took one back.

In the small vestibule of Our Lady of Sorrows church, a poster-sized scorecard advertised *A Night at the Races* in St. Thomas Hall. He took it down and tore it in two, placing the pieces face-forward against the wall. His hands were shaking, his heart thumped with purpose and fear, but he felt better than he did after fifteen minutes of exercises. Kneeling in a wooden pew, he tried to think nothing: no nights at the races, no guitars and Bach cantatas and stained glass, no

Fermi labs and telescopes, no curlicued Father Huntly—who meant well, *but.*

A soft rain was falling, strengthening in gusts. The dark church smelled of damp wood and flowers. The old priest stared at the sanctuary lamp, burning red as an anthurium, and found himself wondering if he could hear that old leak in the roof. He wondered what he should do when it was light. Slip away and go home? And then what?

The dawn was balmy and sweet, rain cloud breaking into opalescent pink floats. In the plumeria grove, murmuring doves pecked at wet blossoms covering the earth, like snow, he thought, or pieces of paper.

Waiting, he let the idea form, warming him. Could he? A snowstorm of letters? A campaign? Letters everywhere, one after another, *ta, ta, ta, ta*— With his new pen! To bishops, newspapers, parishioners, and then they could write— Father LaClaire, *voyageur* and agitator. If not China, why not Green Bay!

He hurried to the Toyota and, opening the door, saw his packet with something taped to it—a yellow piece of paper with unfamiliar handwriting, then Father Huntly's signature followed by a happy face drawn in a circle. He read the words several times, trying to absorb their meaning, but he could only wonder how Father Huntly had read it all so soon. Stayed up all night, maybe? But Father Huntly hadn't read it, it seemed, and didn't intend to. Nor did he want Father LaClaire to regret anything later, particularly regret writing things that should perhaps be kept in confidence. And as he, Father Huntly, wouldn't feel comfortable in the role of Father LaClaire's confessor, he hoped Father LaClaire—overwrought though he might have been the night before—would understand the necessity of his returning the packet. He was also sorry they didn't see eye to eye "on things," but Father LaClaire might be reassured to know permission had been granted for all these changes and innovations. "Forgive this note," he concluded, "but I find it hard to say no and hurt people's feelings. I'm hoping we'll be able to chat a bit in the morning, after Mass."

The old priest looked toward the quiet rectory, the church, the still village, then got in the Toyota. Driving, he heard Tomas saying *ta, ta, ta, ta,* then raising his palms like a visionary. Heard Michael's tearful voice—I can't talk to him, yeah? He wants— He wants too much!

And his own voice coming back to him as he'd addressed Father Huntly the night before, wanting too much—still! The irony, the mockery of it wounding: *Oh please. Things have to change. Change is necessary.*

SEVEN

He drove over the buried village of Kapoho toward the rising sun, passing red and black cinder cones and the remains of a large crater now sheltering a lush farm. Reaching a plain of lava, he remembered the story of a lighthouse keeper who refused to leave his light in 1968, even though it was in the direct path of a grinding, smoldering wall of clinker-like lava. Madame Pele, the lighthouse keeper believed, would spare the lighthouse, and so the man had stood there, facing the advancing, smoking wall. At the last minute the massive flow broke in two, branching around the lighthouse before dropping to the sea and sending up geysers of steam and gases.

So what does that tell you? the old priest asked himself.

He wasn't sure.

The road narrowed to one lane. Jungle vegetation swept against the Toyota. Rutted tracks led off into the jungle, some posted with hand-lettered signs that said *Kapu!* A few modest houses set in a coconut grove had views of the ocean—sapphire here, with waves exploding against cliffs. Then jungle again. The priest began looking for familiar landmarks, but nothing appeared exactly right. Finally he looked for a spot where the ditch wasn't too deep and where it seemed possible to maneuver through trees. He checked the road ahead. No one. He checked the rear-view mirror. Nothing.

Coming up out of the ditch, the Toyota stalled and rolled back. If anyone saw him, he worried, angled like that, half in and half out of the ditch, what would they think? They'd stop. There'd be a fuss. The Toyota's tires spun on slippery needles and bumped over lava rocks. He was in the woods now, and worrying about a flat tire. But it was easy enough to thread a course through the ironwood pines—turning toward the light, simply, and zig-zagging around stones and shrubs and humps. He thought of the watchdog fishermen out on their rock, and fear came. But maybe he could say he'd just gotten lost, had been partying a little, his face proof—falling-down drunk, is what they'd called it in Wisconsin.

The Toyota suddenly cleared the trees and rolled up a slant of fractured black stone as if wanting to launch itself into nothingness.

Waves pounded against the cliff, sending up fountains of water and spray. His legs were quivering as he held down the brake and carefully shifted into reverse—double checking, then easing up on the pedals. The Toyota slid back into the shade of pines. He got out. The whole cliff was quaking. Or else, he thought, it was him. After each wave came the jingling sound of water spattering down, then a great outrushing as the wave fell back, crashing into another. He went closer to the edge. No trail—that he could see. Nothing but rough triangles of fallen stone all along the cliffs. Waves foamed over great sulphur-colored heads of coral. Salt mist rose like fog. He couldn't remember there being any coral. And where was that causeway leading to the lava spire?

Not the right place at all, he decided. Could he walk along the cliff, keeping an eye out? He looked in one direction, then the other—the same either way—a sheer drop, surging water, and clouds of salt mist. Have a bite to eat, maybe, he told himself, then try. The thought caused him to smile, hurting his face: build up strength for the end. Yet it made sense. If he was going to die alone anyway one day soon, why not as Tomas had? Tomas had known when it would be, and maybe so did he now. Everything fritzing out, Father Huntly thinking him nothing but a crackpot. Young people were sharp. They knew what was what. Some things, anyway. And as for the rest, the packet . . . This thought brought on a muddle of feelings, something telling him to go back to Pahoa; something else, stronger, telling him to stay—done was done.

In the trunk he found a mat and a large beach towel and the rest of his lunch.

The priest opened his eyes. A gaunt young man, very brown and wearing only swimming trunks, sat alongside the mat, watching him. His sun-bleached hair was tied back in a ponytail. Cradled in one arm was a sleeping kitten, a ginger tabby. On the ground nearby was half a papaya with a penknife stuck in it. "All *right!*" this apparition said. "I was wondering when."

The priest's wallet, fallen from his pocket, lay in full view on the mat. The Toyota was still where he'd left it. But where were his keys?

"You want some papaya? Only, you have to watch out for the little wormies." He fed the kitten papaya, digging chunks out with the penknife. "It's all we eat, man. No, I take that back. Bananas, too. I can get you some if you want. You want?"

"Ah, no. Thank you so much. I've just had my lunch."

"It's no trouble, man."

"I'm sure it's not. Thank you all the same."

"Whatcha up to, here?"

"Ah—"

"You one of *them,* or you just lost?"

"No, not lost. Not really."

"Too bad, hey? You don't look like a bad guy, man." He made a series of staccato sounds beginning with the letter *b,* then mimed strangling himself. "You know?"

"Are you camping here?" the priest asked.

"Oh, wow. *Hoo!* Listen to this. They just left her, man. They just go and open the door, then slam and mew, mew, mew, but no more car, no more peeps except me. We do OK. Right?" He lifted the kitten to his face, swung it out an arm's length, then brought it back to his face. "Nerds. Right?"

Please Lord, the priest prayed, don't let him fling the cat into the sea.

The young man placed the kitten on top of his head and it stayed there, front paws splayed over the mess of hair. "*Hoo!*" He lowered it to the pine needles and fed it another chunk of papaya he dug out with his fingers. It ate hungrily and wanted more.

The priest regretted finishing the last cheese sandwich. "Would you like to come with me? You can bring the kitten. We could, ah, stop in Pahoa and get something to eat, then go on to Hilo if you want. Do you have . . . I mean, is there anybody—"

On his back, with the kitten perched on his chest, the young man was chanting the staccato sounds, while the kitten purred, kneading his flesh. The half-eaten papaya, the priest saw, was indeed wormy.

"I'm Father LaClaire. I live over on the Kona side. What's your name?" This cut no ice, the priest realized. "Is it Tom? Or, wait. I bet it's Mark."

"Hoo-*hoo.* That's rich. A-ga!"

"Oh, it's not Aga, is it? It can't be that."

"*Aga!*"

"OK. Aga. Hello. I'm Father John."

"You're a riot, man."

"Not at all. I'm Father John LaClaire. I'm from Wisconsin, originally. Where are you from?"

"Outasight." He sat up, slipping the kitten into his lap, where it rearranged itself. "You don't happen to have a spoon, do you, man?" I could really use a spoon. Had a nice plastic one but now it's gone."

"I have spoons at home."

"Where's that at?"

"Over on the Kona side."

"Oh, well."

"Would you like to come with me?"

"No way. It's nice here. No hassles."

"We could stop and get a meal in Pahoa, and then—"

"Can't, man. Can't leave my mates."

"Here?"

"Want to see something? Watch." He crossed his eyes and stretched his mouth wide open. His head shook with tension. He uncrossed his eyes and closed his mouth. "Ah-ga!" Now you try it."

"Oh, I couldn't."

"Sure. Go ahead."

The priest crossed his eyes and opened his mouth as wide as he could, tearing his cuts. "Ah-ga!" he said. Then, "Ouch."

"Neat, huh? But you don't have a spoon."

"No, I'm sorry—"

"Well, take it easy." He scooped up kitten and papaya.

"Wait!"

The priest was able to follow him until he slipped into the jungle, and the priest sank in spongy, waist-high grass that nearly toppled him. He had to fight his way back to firmer ground. Soon he heard waves again. And there was his wallet. The Toyota. The keys were in his pocket.

Kneeling on the mat and facing the ocean, he said prayers for Tomas, then for the unfortunate soul whose name might or might not be Aga. Something replaced the exhaustion he'd felt earlier—the heaviness still there, but the numbness gone. Everything hurting, everything a pressure point, but some warmth, now, and need. Above all, need. Something unfocused but making him want to embrace each thing in this isolated, haunted place.

He rolled up the mat and folded the towel. He made sure he'd collected his sandwich wrapping and banana peel. For a long time he sat in the Toyota until he sensed no one was going to appear. Just a fishing boat passing quite close to the cliff and going on.

Nearly to the road, he stopped. How could he be so stupid? But it would be too hard to back up all that way. He'd have to walk. From his duffel bag he took out the nylon windbreaker and the sweater; from the trunk he took the mat and towel. These he carried to the cliff, following the scuffed pine needles. He emptied his wallet of most of the money, zipping it into one of the windbreaker's pockets. He placed the clothing and towel at one end of the mat and folded over the other. In the event, he told himself, he hadn't been dreaming.

Sliding patches of sunlight, pine branches humming, waves thudding—and somebody coming, he was sure of it, somebody right there, behind him. He turned, chills rippling through him.

"Aga?"

In the shade of the ironwood pines, no one. "Tomas?" he said more softly. "Is that you?"

Another wave broke, sending up glassy fragments, but that was all.

He looked at the sad pile of things and tried to think. What else? What else?

Roberto, all in white and wearing a starched white cap, stood behind the cash register, making change. A TV mounted on a corner shelf was on loud, a morning talk show. Roberto's wife Anna came through a curtained doorway that led from the family living quarters and the bakery to this public area, both restaurant and dining room for the family. She carried a plate heaped with eggs, toast, and papaya for a young man sitting at a table decorated with a small anthurium in a bud vase. The guy was Aga, the priest thought, amazed. But the long curly hair was too glossy, a clean gold-brown; his manner too sane. Roberto looked up after his customer left and, in his usual sullen way, asked Anna to bring two coffees. Now Anna recognized the priest and bowed a little, smiling. She had gained more weight and walked more slowly than ever, tipping from side to side in her tent dress. The priest wished Roberto had gone for the coffee himself.

Roberto came around the counter and motioned the priest to a table near a curved glass china cabinet filled with lava rocks and photographs of volcanic eruptions, then reached under his apron and took a pack of cigarettes from a shirt pocket. Sit or don't sit, he seemed to say. It doesn't matter to me. To the priest, Roberto appeared like a man for whom even talk was too much trouble. His face was pouchy and sweaty, disinterested. But, the priest supposed, he probably didn't look so hot himself. He sat down.

"Funny thing," Roberto said. "They want you back."

"No."

"Yeah."

"Well, that is strange."

"They think your crazy mo-bettah than his."

"Oh, but *he's* not—" It took a while to understand that Roberto had made a joke.

Anna served their coffee with a plate of warm rice cookies and jam. "Nice to see you, Father."

"And you, Anna. When are you and Roberto going to take a vacation and come visit me?"

This made her giggle. "You ask Roberto, yeah?" She tilted back through the curtains, then came out again to wait on a customer who asked for bread. It pained the priest to see her walking—and she so happy, it seemed, just getting from point to point, as if that were enough. Then he was thinking of the packet, still in the car, and the earlier excitement about writing letters. But if everybody thought he was crazy—

"What?"

"Oh! Sorry! I guess I was just thinking out loud."

Roberto made a small sound, meaning—the priest took it—that he couldn't care less about the Father LaClaires and Father Huntlys and their goofiness. What were they but an import, like the mongoose who was supposed to eat the rats living in the cane fields but didn't and so wound up being just another nuisance. Roberto was sitting down because he needed, just then, a break, not because he had a visitor from the old days. The priest warned himself not to take too much of Roberto's time.

"We got lotsa trouble here now," Roberto said. "Lucky you gone." He reached for a newspaper left on another table and slid it toward the priest. A news photo showed a helicopter that had been fired on by someone with a high-powered rifle. Headlines said state agents were burning marijuana patches back in the jungle. TV noise washed out most of Roberto's words, but the priest caught a few: booby-traps, gangsters, injuries. Soon marijuana would be everywhere, growing wild.

"Roberto—" the priest ventured, when it seemed the baker was through ranting. "I couldn't find the spot. You know. I thought I must be close, but evidently I didn't turn in the right place. Things didn't seem right and—"

"Thanks!" the young man called, leaving. "Great food!"

"Yeah," Roberto said. "Good." He went to the other table and took a bill from under the plate. He showed it to the priest. Ten dollars. "What he had was, oh, dollar-fifty."

"Is *he*—?"

Roberto shrugged. "Who knows. They come in all the time. Lotsa money. Always cash. They want a new truck, they go and buy it. Take the money from here." He slapped his hip.

"Don't tell Father Huntly."

Roberto seemed to like the joke. He sat down again and took out another cigarette, then looked at the priest. His face was more open now, friendly. "You want to go back there?"

"You mean right now?"

Roberto looked away. "Now. Later. I can go now."

"Well, then— I did want to— Do you think I might buy, ah—" He raised the coffee spoon. "Buy this from you and take it along? Oh! And a couple loaves of bread. Yes, that would be good. Then I can get some cheese, maybe, from Mrs. Hakutani. And fish."

Roberto stared at him. "Take," he said finally. "No buy."

"Thank you! And look—I almost forgot! This is for you." The priest put the can of Kona coffee on the table, next to the vase of anthurium.

"We drive your car, yeah?" Roberto said.

Big swells broke, sending up spray. The pinnacle of lava at the end of the narrow causeway reminded the priest of the hot-water radiators in the Wisconsin farmhouse, the way they'd been painted silver. Roberto hadn't said two words all the way out, and now was sitting Buddha-like on pine needles. The priest went close to the edge and knelt down. Sun burned the right side of his face, his neck, his right arm. Salt spray stung his cuts, and the shock of each wave-thud jolted through him. He tried to pray, but the awareness of danger broke all concentration. He tried telling himself that it was really what he wanted, wasn't it?—to be done, finished with it all? Yet he retreated back into the shade and sat down next to the man who, he sensed, had brought him out here to kill him. Dying on his own, slipping away as Tomas had, was one thing, but to encourage someone in terrible temptation—!

"Roberto, I don't have much time left. My health, you know, isn't so hot. I want to tell you how bad I feel, still, about Tomas, his family, everything that happened."

Roberto covered his face with both hands, and when he lowered them, he appeared meaner, angrier.

"Roberto, forgive me, but I must ask. Was there ever—is there, I mean, some curse?"

"Tomas no *kolea ino.*"

Evil bird. "No. I know that. Then there wasn't, you're saying. Really, I don't know how those things work, or even if they do. People get sick naturally. Bodies go haywire. Just like when you had that scare, remember?"

Roberto, looking out over the cliffs, said nothing.

"I'm ashamed to have even thought it."

"Lotsa times Tomas don't eat, yeah?"

"I remember. He'd get sick, then."

"He don't eat to make up for something, I think. Tomas full of sadness."

"To make up for— What?"

"Because he say he was bad priest! The land go bad, the kids. Even his wife he lose. Everything. Because he's bad."

"Oh, my Lord, then you're saying he *did?*"

Roberto shrugged. "Tomas no *kolea ino*. He try an' make you bettah." He pinched shut his eyes. "Only he says he can't. No more power. All gone."

"Make me better? But what happened before that? Did he do something— Something bad? Roberto?"

Roberto looked down. He plucked a stem. He shrugged. "What do I know? I say go ahead. You deserve. You the *kolea ino*. But when you get sick, he tries to make you bettah."

"Roberto, I still don't understand. Didn't he tell you? You were his best friend. You used to sit on the bench, talking and laughing— Didn't he tell you anything?"

The baker shook his head and plucked another stem. "After his wife die, he was lost."

"I know he was." The memory came like sudden pain. *Forgive me,* Tomas had said.

"Yet he never told you—?"

Again the sullen shake of the head. "He try to make you bettah, that he says to me. An' before, he try to make his wife bettah. Tomas a healer, but no, nothing works."

"If he did do something . . . bad, then that, too, is all my fault! Don't you see? That's what so terrible, Roberto!"

Light seemed to wave streaks around them, a net holding each of them still. The priest could almost feel the lava scraping his hands, rushing away from him. How long would he have? A minute or two? More? To die that way, beaten against rocks, smashed, broken, then drowned! His body clenched, but he was able to make a hasty Act of Contrition, then touch Roberto's arm.

"When something like this happens, you know, it can go on and on. Sometimes there's no end to it. The bad work. Oh, Roberto, please— You must try, now, to forgive. I believe he did. Tomas.

Remember? We were right here. He said my name. He gave me a stone, which I still have and treasure. I was no stranger, he said. No evil bird. That's what he said, even though I was! *That* was his power, Roberto— Maybe it came back to him right then!"

The opaque curtains usually swirling around his thoughts and blocking the light were parting, opening on some clear vista: Everything flees the grasping claw but moves into the open hand, making a nest there. "Oh, Roberto. If you want to push me over, I don't care—so much—for myself. Go ahead. I'm ready. Done is done. Only I'm thinking, now, of you. What might happen and keep on happening, who knows! The effects, they could . . . go on and on. Good Lord."

"When you show up today and say you want to come out here, I think, finish up, yeah?"

The priest cringed from the anger in the baker's voice.

"But now what? Now I can't."

The priest felt it again, as he had earlier: the air dense with energy, saturated with invisible form.

—Oh, Tomas.

They found the pile of things left for Aga, still covered by the mat, and the priest added the spoon, the bread, and the groceries from Mrs. Hakutani's. Roberto, watching, said he was crazy for sure.

A mountain range of white cloud crowned the island, obscuring Mauna Loa and Mauna Kea, as he drove back with Roberto, each of them silent. At the farm in the crater, cattle grazed under broad trees. In the papaya groves, gold windfall lay along the rows. Such goofy, improbable trees, it struck him. Homely survivors from some prehistoric time. Knobs of green like giant brussels sprouts. Circlets of palmate leaves. Oddball trees, but sun-encrusted, those leaves. Everything geared to catching light.

He pointed. "The first telescopes, Roberto!"

Beyond the papaya plantations, they came to the humid shade of Tomas's jungle, then sunlight once more, and cane fields flowing green and silver in the trade winds.

"The thing is, we've got so far to go," the old priest said. A confused sadness took hold of him though he felt, still, anointed with light from the moment on the cliffs. There'd be no blitzkrieg of letters now, no pestering Father Huntly. "So far, yet, to *go*. That's the thing!"

"Watch the road, yeah?"

But he wasn't aware of the road, just the vast emerald lake ahead, awash with light.

The Irish name "Higgins," taken in marriage more than twenty years ago, masks Joanna Higgins' background as a fourth-generation Polish-American in the small town of Alpena, Michigan.

Ms. Higgins received a B.A. from Aquinas College in Michigan, an M.A. from the University of Michigan, and a Ph.D. from SUNY-Binghampton. She taught English at a U.S. Air Force Base in England, at Keystone Junior College in Pennsylvania, and at Hilo College and West Oahu College in Hawaii. She returned to Pennsylvania in 1979 and studied with writer John Gardner until his death in 1982.

The Importance of High Places is Ms. Higgins' first published book. Her stories and essays have been published in many journals and anthologies, including *American Fiction, The Best American Short Stories, Four Quarters, Honolulu Magazine, MSS, Passages North, Passages North Anthology,* The Philadelphia *Inquirer* Magazine, *Prairie Schooner,* and *The Writer.* She received the P.E.N. Syndicated Fiction Award in 1984 and a National Endowment for the Arts Fellowship in Literature in 1989.

Joanna Higgins and her husband live in Little Meadows, Pennsylvania, where she spends her time writing, hiking, and sometimes teaching children in the schools about writing. When she's not teaching, she tries to write every day—fiction, essays, plays, and works for children.

Designed by Charles Alexander
at Chax Press in Tucson, Arizona.
Illustrations and cover design by R.W. Scholes.
Titling in Optima
and text in Adobe Minion,
typeset by Charles Alexander.
Printed on acid-free Glatfelter
by Princeton University Press.

MORE FICTION FROM MILKWEED EDITIONS:

Larabi's Ox: Stories of Morocco
Tony Ardizzone

Agassiz
Sandra Birdsell

What We Save for Last
Corinne Demas Bliss

Backbone
Carol Bly

The Clay That Breathes
Catherine Browder

Street Games: A Neighborhood
Rosellen Brown

Winter Roads, Summer Fields
Marjorie Dorner

Blue Taxis: Stories about Africa
Eileen Drew

Circe's Mountain
Marie Luise Kaschnitz
Translated by Lisel Mueller

Ganado Red
Susan Lowell

Tokens of Grace
Sheila O'Connor

The Boy Without a Flag: Tales of the South Bronx
Abraham Rodriguez, Jr.

Cracking India
Bapsi Sidhwa

The Crow Eaters
Bapsi Sidhwa

The Country I Come From
Maura Stanton

Traveling Light
Jim Stowell

Aquaboogie
Susan Straight